The Art of Trespassing

The Art of Trespassing

Edited by Anna Leventhal

Invisible Publishing
Halifax & Montréal

Library and Archives Canada Cataloguing in Publication

The art of trespassing / edited by Anna Leventhal.
Short stories.
ISBN 978-0-9782185-4-6
1. Short stories, Canadian (English). 2. Canadian fiction (English)--
21st century. I. Leventhal, Anna, 1979-
PS8329.1.A78 2008   C813'.010806   C2008-905074-6

Designed by Megan Fildes
Cover and interior illustration by Kit Malo

Typeset in Laurentian by Megan Fildes
With thanks to type designer Rod McDonald

Printed and bound in Canada

Invisible Publishing
Halifax & Montréal
www.invisiblepublishing.com

We acknowledge the support of the Canada Council for the Arts which
last year invested $20.1 million in writing and publishing throughout
Canada.

Invisible Publishing recognizes the support of the Province of Nova
Scotia through the Department of Tourism, Culture & Heritage. We are
pleased to work in partnership with the Culture Division to develop and
promote our cultural resources for all Nova Scotians.

Canada Council   Conseil des Arts
for the Arts   du Canada

NOVA SCOTIA
Tourism, Culture and Heritage

Preface

This began as a collection of stories about infrastructure. The idea was to gather a bunch of writing on systems and frameworks to sketch out a kind of map of the lines that connect and repel us. But what became clear as the collection developed is that the story doesn't lie so much in the map itself as in how it's used—the paths worn, the spaces taken.

The most interesting stories are often the ones of things being where you don't expect them. *The Art of Trespassing* emerged as an anthology of writing that claims its own space, usually where it knows it shouldn't. Some of these pieces are literally about trespassing: a couple of kids rifle through the charred remains of a former suburban dreamhouse, or find an uneasy solace in the guts of a squatted factory. Others approach the idea of "sneaking in" more obliquely: sickness and substance intrude on bodies, bodies intrude on each other. Some consider trespassing on a larger scale: the toxic bloom of colonialism, the swell and fail of cities. All of them share a sense of breaking new ground, or finding new ways of crossing old.

We hope you enjoy this anthology, though it will probably not do you as much good as a map, a compass, and a crowbar.

Anna Leventhal, Editor

Anna Leventhal

The Land and How it Lay

Caraway-on-Rye began as a prairie crossroads, the X where the west and southbound caravan routes intersected. Pilgrim's Last Chance, the neighbouring farmers called it, or Floating Kneecap after the nearby Knee River, or Devil's Psoriasis on account of the drought. The first settlers to stake their tent pegs in its red hide were two rival families who found the land less than hospitable but also less hostile than their native Lithuania (or was it Romania?). Still, sometimes when she looked at the crisp blue bed sheet overhead, homesickness would prick Anya Kouslouski with its baby-garter teeth. She had lost her first child to the prairie, and since the land was too firmly packed for grave digging, she kept its little body in a leather pouch, which she kept meaning to send down the Knee but somehow never did. The dry air had preserved it and it sat stowed under the bed like a jar of pickled beets or a dirty secret. If she were back home, her mother and sisters would have taken care of the burial, swaddled the baby in a tablecloth and sung the family chant over it, their eyes rolling in their heads like frightened horses. No one chastised Anya, then, when she occasionally plopped down in the middle of a field and started making dust-angels, and sometimes didn't come home until after dessert.

On the north side of the river were the snake ranchers. Their children proudly bore on their arms the sore red spots and bite marks, the telltale punctuation of their trade. They learned early how to tell a common garter from a poisonous mamba, and the slow studies were buried under cairns of river rock drawn from the Knee (apart from Anya's baby, of whom it was said "waters shall not separate and stone cannot keep down").

On the south side were their old rivals the ladder merchants. They called their northward cousins scale-mongers and cold-bloods, and when Toma Paulescu sliced the top of his middle finger off with a lathe, he hid the evidence under a juniper bush and told everyone "one of them neckless monsters" bit it off. Ranch children took to chanting "big fat ladderoo where you gonna climb to", and in retaliation the merchant kids stashed their enemies' toys on the highest thing they could find—a young sycamore just over five feet tall.

In summer the ladder merchants' sweat would mix with the varnish on their work, and in winter the snake ranchers would squat like mother hens on their numbed stock, hoping to keep the snakes from forming a ball of intertwined bodies, a knot from which they would never wriggle free. When the first power lines shot up like alien cornstalks overhead, the richer families of each camp rushed out to buy themselves electric cooling boxes and heat lamps respectively, while the poorer had to make do with special sweat-resistant varnish and the occasional red, punctured rump.

The first inter-camp marriage, between Lina Kouslouski (merchant) and Paul Tomasescu (rancher), took place under a bevy of heat lamps that caused some stray snake-stock to writhe themselves nearly unconscious with pleasure. The bride wore snakeskin boots, and her family presented the groom with a beautiful new ladder made of imported oak, with silver inlay grips and the couple's initials engraved in the top rung. Later that night Lina dreamed uneasily of a sack of gold stashed on a high shelf, just out of reach. Paul, for his part, lay awake and thought to himself that there was no stranger sensation than having a pair of snakeskin boots rubbing up against one's earlobes.

Years later, Lina Tomasescu emerged from her modest house in what would later become downtown Caraway-on-Rye to a strange sight. Her wedding ladder, whose restoration her husband had devoted himself to since his retirement, stood leaning against a tree in the backyard. Wrapped through and around its rungs was a huge boa constrictor, the kind her neighbours had been breeding for fun in their root cellar. Something about the snake's spiral form and the way it embraced the ladder like a lover seemed primordial and somehow evil to her, caused her to shudder and wrap her arms around her chest.

That is not a standard-type animal, she said to herself. The snake's blank stare made her turn back inside and shake her sleeping husband awake, but by the time they went back to the yard there was only the ladder, its half-coat of new varnish already dulling in the sun.

Her discovery of the Deadly Not-Animal, or D.N.A., as she took to calling it, became a subject of ridicule for the townspeople, who chalked it up to the history of female hysteria and "dry womb" in her family.

The early train routes brought a passel of land hungry prospectors, draft dodgers, and religious fanatics. One night Big Hand Skender (who was not yet called Big Hand) and his brothers lurked in the bushes outside an oilcloth tent on which the words Church of the Redeeming Blood were painted. From inside they could hear yelps and dark, earthy sounds that reminded Skender of walking past his parents' bedroom in the middle of the night on the way to the outhouse. When the brothers saw Jericha Johansson leaving the tent, they followed behind her, whispering taunts and threats:

Your momma bought you from Gypsies; when you're ripe she's gonna take you to market and sell you to Old Man Gurdebeke for a donkey and a pair of dice.

The next morning Skender shook out his pants, muddy and creased from the night before, only to have a snake shoot out from one of the pockets and bite him on the thumb. His hand swelled up until it looked like a catcher's mitt, and not even his mother's chamomile balm could make it go down. From then on Big Hand Skender insisted on wearing only pockets with zippers, which his mother would have to sew onto his trousers herself.

Wars extracted young men from the town like malevolent dentists pulling healthy teeth. Every year the ticker-tape parade became smaller and smaller, until one day Bart (Bartosz) Oneschuk stepped lively from the regiment headquarters, blue serge uniform with white piping freshly pressed and medals gleaming, to find he was the only soldier there. The high school marching band goggled in silence. Someone dropped a high hat. Undeterred, Bart strode on down Main Street, his knees popping up and down in time to unheard music. The cheerleading Pep-ettes followed behind him, executing cartwheels and handstands and pirouettes, past the row houses lining the otherwise empty street.

The snake pits were a hail mary business venture on the part of the Thomas (formerly Tomasescu) family, who had fallen on hard times since the reptile rights movement made people feel bad about buying the hand-tooled snakeskin boots and purses Tyvek Thomas would sweat over in his workshop.

   Guilt, the gift that keeps on taking, Tyvek liked to say. In fact his own name originated from a similar such gift—at his birth his own father's conscience pricked as he thought about passing on his sterile, WASPified surname. He watched his sweat-sticky, doped-up wife cradle their son and wondered if his family hadn't been rash to change their name during the war, in order "to keep the peace". Now they had nearly nothing left in the family of their native Romania (or was it Lithuania?). His eye roamed over a construction site outside the hospital window, fell on a word he took for the name of the construction company, a good name from the old country. And thus Tyvek Thomas, last of the Tomasescu line, was named after a brand of flashspun polyethylene sheeting.

The snake pits lay about a half a kilometre outside the city limits, on a road that decades before had been a main artery feeding highway traffic into the city, but had since fallen into disuse. Only a few scabby stores and chain restaurants still clung to its sides. Tourists in spray-painted vans and field-tripping kids in yellow school buses would roll up to the Welcome Booth, pay the entrance fee, and crowd the edges of the pits in which hundreds, thousands of snakes lived in an apparent eternal game of Twister.

What do they do? wide-eyed kids would ask their teachers or parent-guardians.

Whatever it is, they're doing it now.

Business chugged along steadily until the Kozlowsky family (formerly Kouslouski, who themselves had suffered a downturn in ladder sales since the invention of the elevator) bought the abandoned Buggy Burger across the road. They registered the name Kozmic Pets, painted the storefront in zebra stripes, and hung a sign in the window that read, menacingly, Half Off Gerbils. Now when the buses arrived, the tourists and school kids would scorn the scaled attractions and stroll down the road for more cuddly delights. They handled crusty-eyed kittens and wormy rabbits, cooing when the animals licked their faced, and when a rash of conjunctivitis broke out among the Grade 5 class at Adder Elementary, Tyvek smirked and yanked his niece's ear.

I feel the wind about to change, yessir.

They were standing at the edge of one of the two snake pits, tossing in baby mice by the handful. His niece watched a snake snap up a mouse like a piece of popcorn. Tyvek continued.

Yokels rather look at disease-mongering mammals, fine by me. They'll get their due. Nothing a snake can give you you haven't already got.

God, uncle Ty, his niece said. Give it up. They just want to be free. She didn't know if she was talking about the snakes or the yokels.

Don't I know it. He sighed and dangled a baby mouse by its knobby tail. I like the cut of your jib, he said to it, you get to live. But he chucked it into the snake pit anyway.

Joseph Bonavich stood outside the Cold Blood Café, taking hesitant puffs from a roll-yer-own as he waited for the rest of his band to show up. In the corner of the café window was a small mimeographed flyer that read SNAKS + LADERS: TONIGHT $3 o.b.o. The bass player, a one-time war resistor from Minneapolis who went by the designation Cooch, showed up dragging a Red Flyer wagon with his instrument balanced on top.

Oboe? Cooch said, jerking his head at the sign. We don't have no damn oboe.

It stands for… Joseph started to explain.

I know what it stands for, Cooch said. Jesus-bleeding hick town. He pulled a small leather pouch from his back pocket and took a swig from it. Joseph looked around nervously. Sometimes on his walks around town he would wear a big pair of headphones that weren't actually plugged into anything—the cord ran into the empty pocket of his distressed-leather jacket. His girlfriend said the headphones looked stupid, but he kept wearing them anyway, unsure of why, only that it seemed to keep the swirling colours at the edge of his vision under control. His great-great-grandmother had been a noted lunatic, so Joseph kept careful watch over himself, checking for eccentricities the way a gardener checks for weevils.

Want some, Bonervich? Cooch asked, swinging the leather pouch around.

It was during the big flood of the Garamond administration that Anya Kouslouski's baby finally came back. The old Paulescu farmhouse, right on the bank of the Knee, was sodden up to its doorknobs. Teams of high-school kids showed up to sandbag; when they saw the building rising out of the bilge water like a mirage or a miracle they laughed and went off for a smoke break. Mayor Meyer Skrowaczewski announced that it looked like the Caraway Dike was going to hold, which meant that most of the houses in Caraway-On-Rye would pull through just fine, unless they were right on the riverbank or very unlucky. Meanwhile the elderly Paulescus were moved into a vacant room in the legion hall until their home was liveable again. Once the water receded, their abandoned farmhouse became the spot where kids from Caraway High would go to get stoned and fumble with each others' buttons up against the spongy walls. Georgia Papapolous thought the old house was creepy, and it brought out an allergic flush in her cheeks that the boys mistook for arousal, but she went around anyway because Mikey Rainer had promised her her first hit of acid.

She and Mikey sat in the rotted-out doorway waiting for Mikey's dealer, an old burnout whose name was Joe but who everyone called Boner for some probably dumbass reason. Be cool, Mikey said when the swinging arc of Joe's flashlight came jigging over the hill, Boner's kind of a head case.

What goes on, Mike, Joe said when he was in hollering distance, hey who's this, the Caraway Dyke?

Bite me, Georgia said but it came out as a mumble. Joe brought out a film canister and he and Mikey started talking business. Georgia though she saw something perched in the old sycamore on the hill, maybe a stranded kitten or an owl resting before the hunt.

To-whit to-whit to-whoo, she said softly, and started toward the tree. The owl didn't fly away as she approached it. It was oddly white and luminous, and as she got closer and closer it changed shape, an amoebic mass that pulled itself out, taffy-like, into arms, a sunken head, and one tiny, dangling foot. Her scream drew Mikey and Joe up the hill, squelching and cursing through the rancid mud.

What the hell?! Jesus christ, what is it? She closed her eyes instinctively as Joe flashed the light up into the branches.

Oh for fuck's... it's a plastic bag. Washed up there in the freaking flood. Jesus, you on something? Joe shone his flashlight in her eyes and she glared at the red spot where his head should have been. Whoever sold it to you, they ripped you off good, you know that? He had dropped his roll of acid in a mud puddle and seemed to be spoiling for a fight.

Okay, George, maybe we should split, yeah? Mikey was dancing awkwardly and tugging at her sleeve, trying to disguise the fact that he had wet his pants a little. It was the first time he had called her George. Georgia looked at him, his face a spotty blur in front of the dark green backdrop of the river, then turned and walked away down the hill, toward town. She knew what she had seen.

There came a time when no one could remember ever having seen a snake. Were there snakes here? Townspeople leaning into parking meters and sipping from fountains smiled to themselves and joked with each other about snakes, but it was purely abstract, like joking about God or kidney disease. Even the idea of snakes started to go fuzzy in the town's mind, its edges warping like a waterlogged magazine. Granny Krieghof went into the cellar for a jar of her homemade pickled beets, and came up again shouting I seen one! I seen a snake! But on further inspection it turned out to be an old potato chip bag stuffed with used tissue paper. Granny couldn't recall how it might have got there in the first place.

That ain't what a snake looks like anyhow, Bobby Robertson Jr. scoffed, everyone knows Granny's brain got scrambled when her son died in the Gulf.

Oh yeah, said his older brother, what makes you so smart? What do they look like?

Like... Bobby Jr. paused. Kind of long, and round all around, and skinny, with big sharp teeth at one end, long metal ones, and you use it to make a pile of leaves before winter... He trailed off as his brother started to pummel him in the arm.

That's not a snake, that's a lawnmower, fathead.

We burned the old ladder workshop down because it stank. There must have been a hundred years' worth of dead rats under the floor and boy did they make an ungodly stench. Hell's own beer-fart, Crazy Ronald Martinez called it. Actually, in truth we burned it because everyone knows that ladders make the prettiest fires. Oh, if you could have seen it! Those inverted Vs all in flames like a living cardiogram.

Of course we had to soak them in kerosene first; even then they seemed less to burn than to smoke angrily, like the old women at the shopping centre before we tore it down. Finally Mayor Meyer Skrowaczewski's son Ilya threw a jug full of something through the window. There was a pause, then a loud *fump* that was less a sound than a feeling in your teeth, then the ladders all started burning and twisting at once. We had a pretty good idea then of what eternal damnation might look like, not that we believed in it or anything.

What was in that jug? someone asked. Ilya just shrugged. Something I learned overseas.

It was funny, though—right before the workshop collapsed in on itself, and a rush of sparks flew at us making us cross our arms over our faces, and Lydia Burton's hairsprayed bangs caught on fire, just before all that happened we could have sworn we saw something like a thousand snakes, maybe more, come churning out from under the building and roil over the singed grass, making for the woods. Once Lydia's hair got tamped out with a handful of dirt a few of us went over to investigate, but it was too hot, too blinding, and we shielded our eyes from the embers and talked of going home to our cats and lovers and filing cabinets. But maybe it was snakes and not rats. Now wouldn't that be something.

Sean Michaels

Bluebirds

I went back to Montréal for Christmas. I thought maybe it was time for me to settle down. I put on my old winter coat and maybe it felt like home. Maybe like warmth, maybe like home; I wasn't sure if they were the same thing. I went to my sister's and picked up my nephew, who is very small and who catches snowflakes on his tongue. I took him to the subway and held his hand on the escalator. We took the metro to Ste-Catherine and got out and stood by the side of the road with everyone else. I put him on my shoulders. I was trying to decide if this kind of life felt normal to me. Standing with a crowd at Ste-Catherine, in Montréal, in

Québec, in Canada, with Sam on my shoulders. It had been six days since I had opened my suitcase and I was beginning to forget what it looked like.

The parade went by. People were dressed in red and green. There was a giant candy cane. There were elves. Sam cheered in the way that people with small mouths cheer. I patted his foot. We both caught snowflakes on our tongues.

Santa Claus was gliding by us on his motorized sleigh, waving, when he was shot. I heard a snap, a snap like when you twist open a beer, and then Santa was falling like a sack full of coal. I think some people screamed but the rest of us didn't understand what we were seeing and we didn't move. The sleigh moved right past us and kept going.

Sam was young enough that it didn't matter to him, that Santa Claus had suddenly straightened and fallen. We left before people panicked too seriously. We had hot chocolates at the Panther Café. I made Sam teach me what a panther was. The television news was covering the assassination of Santa Claus but I was just trying to pay attention to what a panther was.

I left a couple of days later.

I was twenty-four when I started travelling. I started late. Most people who get the travel bug start when they're eighteen. The hostels are filled with poets, all eighteen years old, with dirty shoes. They sit in the lounges and try to sound bored as they talk to Fort Lauderdale co-eds about the cities of Buda and Pest.

But I was twenty-four. I had only been outside North America once before, with a girl named Charlie. She wanted to visit the south of France so we flew over there and rented a car and I drove through fields and cornfields in a green Citroën. For two weeks we dipped croissants in little dishes of raspberry jam. We sat in the long heat of restaurant windows and had nothing to say.

I didn't see the point of travelling, then. We had come all that way only to share the same touches and for me to see the same look in her eyes. When we got back to Montréal I put my passport in a drawer and didn't take it out again for two years.

When I travel I stay in hotels. I sleep on king-size beds. I walk into the room and I toss my small leather suitcase onto the bed and then I lie down beside it. The suitcase smells of cinnamon, from Istanbul. And wood smoke, from Dover. And cherries and straw, I don't know why. I lie beside my suitcase with my shoes on and if it's cold I roll into the covers.

The time I'm talking about, when I went with Sam to the parade and then left, I went to a town called Bluebird. I went because of the name. I flew from Montréal into Phnom Penh and hired a driver, a guy called Maurice, to drive me in his purple taxi the three hours to Bluebird. I had seen the name when I was in Hong Kong, on a map of Buddhist sites. I had written it down. *Bluebird, Thailand.*

I was expecting a village made out of sticks or something but Bluebird was made out of concrete. There was one road, also made out of concrete. The sky was the colour of red dirt. People in Bluebird wore grey overalls and peaked caps. They worked at a factory that made battery-powered fans. All the people walking down Bluebird's one street were blowing themselves with one of these battery-powered fans. I went into a store and bought one. I also bought a can of sugarcane juice and I opened it as I walked along a row of chattering trees. My t-shirt was sweated through and the locals stared at me, the Canadian in Bluebird, so I nodded to them each in turn.

"How'd it get the name Bluebird?" I asked Maurice on the way.

"I don't know," he said.

Outside the factory people were smoking. On the wall there was some graffiti I couldn't read.

I left Canada four years ago because I wanted to see Big Ben and Buckingham Palace and the Thames river. I wanted not to be able to buy maple syrup or Coffee Crisp at the grocery store. I wanted to meet a Cockney.

I packed light. When I arrived at Heathrow I stood in the convenience store by the exit, staring at the bottles of water. All the labels were unfamiliar. I fell asleep in the cab into the city. When I woke up the driver was singing along to a song I didn't know. Nobody was wearing shorts, even though it was August. There were shops called *Woolworths* and *Boots*. The buses were double decker and red.

Buckingham Palace was closed. I put my hand in the fountain. I walked to Primrose Hill. I drank some water from a bottle. I had some tea on Regent Street. I tried a scone. At four twenty one in the afternoon I saw Big Ben. It was a different time in Montréal. I thought of some of the people I knew there and wondered what they were doing.

When I felt like it was time to leave London I went to Manchester, where there were famous rock bands whose music I didn't even know. And from Manchester to Newcastle, because I liked the name. And I went to Stonehenge and to the seaside and then took a train to Edinburgh. I slept in king-size beds beside my suitcase and tried very hard to hold onto the sound of Princes Street bagpipes, to make them something I could carry with me for the rest of my life.

There didn't seem to be any blue birds in Bluebird. All the birds were brown. They sat on the road pecking at muddy puddles as big moths, like flying birthday cards, gathered round the flowers. A haggard American flag flew below the Thai one outside the convenience store. Two young men were squatting, spitting tobacco.

"Yes?" said one of them to me.

"Hi," I said.

"Lost?"

"No," I said.

I stood there for a little while, drinking my sugarcane juice.

The other young man was squinting at me. He nodded towards the flag. "American?" he asked.

"No. Canadian."

He seemed impressed by this.

"French?" he said.

I didn't know how to answer this. In Canada, I was English.

"Yes," I said.

Then the man smiled and he began to speak in over-grown French, wildly conjugated, *r*s purred like an alleycat. He told me about Bluebird, the hand-held-fan town, the spot in the atlas that was nothing until two American G.I.s swaggered up with a map and a ballpoint; and the way "Bluebird" sounds like the Thai for "tandem bicycle". I did not understand the French word for "tandem bicycle" but he stood up with his friend and they acted it out, wheeling in mid-air, spitting tobacco in unison.

Down the block at the factory, a bell began to ring. The sound cut right through everything. I finished my can of sugarcane juice. The two men began to saunter back across the street. Their shoes kicked up dust.

"Come back in three hours," one of them said to me, the one who had asked if I was lost. "We drink together."

"Okay," I said. At first it was tentative but then I said it again, letting my voice communicate the happiness I felt at being invited. "Okay," I said. I picked up my suitcase. "Three hours."

The best hamburger I've ever had was in Tokyo. The best falafel, in Paris. The best popsicle was in Fanfarlo, outside Brasília. The brightest stars were in Norway, the hottest day in Bangalore and the coldest in Irkutsk. Or maybe the coldest was in Montréal, four years ago, March, when I decided to leave and I walked home with my coat open, breath puffing into clouds around me, and shivering, ice forming at my eyes.

I went to London, to Manchester, to Newcastle, to Edinburgh—and then kept on going. Kept moving, like I had somewhere to be. That first trip I travelled for thirteen months. When I went back to Montréal I saw my mother, my father, my sister, my great aunts. I met my nephew, Sam, who was very small. There was an election on and I had no idea who to vote for. My favourite bar had closed. I ate a bagel with cream cheese. On the street I saw some old friends and they looked older. I took a spring breath and I left again. Eastern Europe, Russia, India. I travelled by airplane, bus, train. I bought a bicycle in Kashmir and rode it through the gardens. I went wherever I wanted to go. When I saw something that didn't make sense to me I asked about it until it made sense. There is something clear in a passport stamp, a railway schedule, the handshake of a stranger. I spent one night in Afghanistan, near where they think apples were invented. The old woman at the hotel sang Elvis Presley songs. I woke to cathedral bells, to rooster crows, to the prayers that buzzed from minarets. I found a small frog and I carried her in my pocket across the border from Bangladesh to West Bengal, on the night-train. Near Calcutta I let her go and she sat in the grass for almost ten minutes, beautiful, and not leaving.

I had two changes of clothes. I washed my things in hotel sinks, let them dry on strings over my bed. At first I carried a couple of books but I finished them and gave them to some kids in Inverness and I didn't buy any more. I bought maps at train stations.

I went to Montréal for a week and it was New Year's and nothing happened at midnight. Then I went to South America and to Western Europe, and down into Africa, and kissed a girl in Senegal and didn't miss Montréal, didn't miss anything about it, didn't miss the snowfall, or the sunshine, or text messages.

I went back for Christmas. I went to the Santa Claus Parade. Then I went to Bluebird.

I had three hours to kill so I made my way to the Buddhist temple. I followed the signs, hammered into the marshy grass. The symbol for 'Buddhist temple' was a human hand with its fingers folded in a particular way.

The path led around a pond and then straight into a thicket of ferns and rubber trees. In Brazil someone had shown me how you can cut off a sliver of rubber tree with your pen knife, and then take the white wood and chew on it. My suitcase knocked against the tree trunks as I walked. Through the breaks in the canopy you could see brown birds flitting across the sky.

The walk got steep at the moment I expected it to get steep. I waved away insects at the moment I expected to wave away insects. Travelling, you learn the world's general truths. If you sleep on king-sized beds next to your suitcase there is no need to worry about the specific truths, the edged ones. I understood this walk through the trilling trees and up.

When I was twenty three years old I felt I had figured things out. I had never been to London but I knew a lot of things. My parents had a Ford pick-up truck. I lay in the flatbed and looked at the Milky Way. I imagined where my friends would be in five years, and where I would be. I imagined Mr. Carville, my old shop teacher, coming into the store and buying a cabinet I had built. "You built this?!" he would say. I could hear it so clearly. Or the crackle of my parents' voices down the line, and us telling them we were having a baby. In two years, three maybe.

A tallboy of 50 sat between us in the truck. We were taking turns drinking it.

"There's an island in Japan where the beach is full of stars," I said.

"Isn't Japan already an island?" said Robbie.

"It's an island off of the island," I said. "The sand is made of these tiny shells, small as pinheads, but shaped like stars."

"What do they call it?" she asked.

"Call what?"

"The sand."

"They call it star sand," I said. "And there are these wild cats, small and wild cats, with bushy tails."

"But what do they call it in Japanese?"

"The sand?"

"Yeah."

"I don't know," I said.

"You don't know a lot of things," she said. She got up on her elbow and drank from the beer.

It got steeper. A trail that was barely there and yet there. There was a small pile of stones—a shrine or a grave—and I thought about putting my suitcase down beside it. I hefted the suitcase and carried it in my arms like I was carrying a small child. I could feel the heat on my arms and eyelids. I saw a snake shush through the undergrowth, beautiful and quiet and emerald. I came to an old stone staircase and climbed. It led to the top of a hill and then there was a path along the cliff's edge. Letters had been carved with a stick into the earth. The Thai words looked like signatures.

Later I went back with the two men from the convenience store to the hut where they lived. It was made of plywood and corrugated iron, with a hole drilled into the wall for the electrical wires. There was a black & white TV, a small fridge, a stove, a CD player with tiny tinny speakers, but no running water. When we arrived they put on some surf guitar music and we cracked open some beers and we sat on cushions on the floor.

We spoke in French.

"How long have you been in Thailand?" said the man who had invited me. His name was Archy.

"I flew into Phnom Penh this morning."

This surprised them. Archy laughed. He slapped the ground with his open hand.

"You came straight to Bluebird?" said the other man. His name was Inerane.

"Yes."

"Why here?"

"I liked the name."

"Bluebird," Archy said. He made a smaller version of the gesture from earlier, that had meant 'tandem bike'. We laughed together. "Just because you liked the name," said Archy. "This makes no sense. You are crazy."

"Have you ever been to New York?" asked Inerane.

"Yes," I said.

"Los Angeles?"

"Yes."

"Paris?"

"Yes," I said.

"Eiffel Tower," Archy said.

"Have you ever been to Mumbai?" Inerane asked.

"I've been to Mumbai."

Inerane grinned. He was missing his two front teeth. "North Pole?"

I smiled back. "No."

"Still one place!" he said.

I smiled. I smiled at the floor.

"To live in Montréal," said Archy. "It must be amazing. It must be—" he used a word I didn't understand. "Work, and money, and cars."

"Snow," said Inerane.

"Yes and snow. Lots of snow, eh?"

"Yes," I said.

"I love snow. I imagine it. Like feathers."

"You should go to Montréal."

"Yes?" said Archy. "Stay with you?"

"Yes," I said. "For sure."

"Truly?" He clapped his friend on the shoulder. "Inerane too? Probably not, eh? This—?" He used a Thai word I didn't understand. "Lots of pretty girls in Montréal."

"There are pretty girls everywhere," I said.

"Pretty girls everywhere!" Archy said, happily. "Like rain."

"Starlight," said Inerane.

"Do you have a wife?" asked Archy.

"No," I said.

"Why not?"

"It's complicated," I said. "At home things are very complicated."

"How complicated?" said Archy. "Here it is complicated. In Montréal: easy. Love girl, marry girl, happy."

The summer before I left, I would go with a girl called Nina to Jean-Talon Market and walk in sneakers over fruit-stains, and eat ice-cream, and I could name every kind of feta cheese in the vats of feta because my father was Greek and he taught me the differences. Four months later my pockets were full of chestnuts and the puddles spelled Nina's name out on the ground, in ice, and I didn't know what my memories even meant.

"Maybe," I said.

Inerane shrugged. He played with the ring on his finger.

I followed the path around the cliff face. Down below were miles and miles of jungle, and hills, and wreaths of mist like smoke as it leaves someone's mouth. Greens, whites and greys. You could slip into this jungle and no one would ever find you and the land would accept you like it was the easiest thing in the world.

I didn't know what to expect, climbing the path to the temple. I didn't know if at the summit there would be a tower or a monument, or a golden house—some kind of pagoda. I thought maybe at the top there would be nothing at all. The ruins of something beautiful.

The path turned and widened into a small grove of birches. When I was growing up we had a cottage near Trois Rivières and in the summer we'd sit with our backs to the birches, the trunks firm and real, and we'd tear off the bark and write on it like it was paper. In Asia the birches are different. They are like ghosts. I went through the slender birches, the translucent birches, and then I was stepping on pine-needles and the air was cool, as if I wasn't in Thailand any more. I could smell the scent of pine needles; a smell like mint and rosemary and whiskey. There's a secret smell in places like this, a moist and secret smell, and it doesn't smell like bodies but it has the same quality of smell as the smell of bodies, when they're close and folded against you.

Archy got up to get some more beers from the fridge. He twisted the caps off the bottles.

"I saw Santa Claus get shot," I said.

"Who?" said Inerane.

"Santa Claus," I said. "Ho ho ho. Père Noël."

"Jesus?" said Archy.

I could not believe that they did not know Santa Claus. "Santa Claus!" I said. I was dehydrated. "Come on! Santa! The fat man with the beard and the red suit. In the…" I did not know the French word for 'sleigh'. Or 'reindeer'. "The man with the deer, and the flying car. Giving children presents on Christmas."

"In Montréal?" said Inerane.

"I would like a flying car," said Archy.

"No," I said. "It's a children's story."

"Fiction."

"Yes."

"But was he shot or was he not shot?"

"He was shot."

I think I must have been a little drunk.

"This is not clear to me," said Inerane.

"It is perfectly clear. It is clear as day. He was dressed up like Santa Claus and he was shot."

Inerane and Archy looked at each other.

"Santa!" I said.

My arms were tired and I put down the suitcase for a moment. My fingers brushed against its leather and it felt like the nape of a woman's neck. I raised my eyes and there through the canopy was the face of Anavisevara, the vast head of a Buddhist saint, a beautiful basalt statue bigger than everything and one hundred feet tall and with an orange tree growing from its forehead. It looked out onto the countryside with great, grey eyes. Its lips were parted and I imagined it smiling. My suitcase was at my feet and I did not want to pick it up. I wanted to stay with this vast, kind face and wait until I could hear and feel it breathing, until I was part of its constituency and welcomed into its gaze. I wanted to stay. I felt an awe for the village of Blue-bird, the jungle below us, the ten million moths who in nighttime climbed and fluttered and swam around the face of Anavisevara, like its dreams.

I stayed on the mountain until it was getting dark. I thought of the men down below and the way they had said "Come back in three hours". I thought of Sam. Returning down the path it was suddenly very cold. There were nocturnal animals on the path with me. Part-way down I put my suitcase on a boulder and opened the clasps. I took out a sweater and a flashlight.

"Good up there?"

"Where?"

"Up the hill."

"Oh," I said. "Yes. How did you know I went?"

Archy shrugged. "Big head, eh?"

I agreed.

"Holy place."

We drank from our beers.

"Ho ho ho'?" said Inerane, finally

"Ho ho ho' is what Santa Claus says. It's his laugh."

"It is the sound that the machine makes at the factory," said Inerane, "spitting smoke. Now I will call it Santa Claus."

"He was shot," I said.

"One day the machine, also, will break," said Inerane.

As I came down the path I passed the flashlight beam through the air and saw the moving of ten thousand wings.

Michelle Sterling

Desist

Joe Pickles, creator and owner of Surf 'n Turf, and occasional Mr. Turf understudy, had downsized his staff to the essentials—one canteen attendee, one lifeguard; and a single Mr. Turf mascot, recently attacked with a steak knife by a gang of teenagers smacked up on Fluky beer. The lawsuit was pending, but as Joe Pickles crushed a tab of Desist with the bottom of a bottle of BBQ sauce, he refused to believe that this was the end.

He took a sip of coffee and spat it back in the cup. Kitty litter. Strong, acidic, unchanged. Why had everything begun to taste like piss? He thought about this for a moment and placed both feet on the corner of the desk. Fuck it. He stamped the heels of his crocodile skin loafers on the desk's surface, knocking one of the glass steak-shaped paperweights to the ground. The paperweight smashed to shards. Doesn't matter. There were more steak-shaped paperweights where that came from. An entire storage cube, in fact. He made a note in his agenda to get the steak-shaped paperweights infomercial on the air again and using one of the larger pieces of glass, he arranged the powdered Desist into a straight line.

Joe tore off a corner of a take-out menu and rolled it into a cylinder. He snorted the line and fluttered his eyelids. When people had told him that waterslides and steaks were not a practical combination, he hadn't wavered, and developed fifty acres of property on the edge of the Tip-Top Treatment Facility. It wasn't the most central location and on days the wind blew northward, the standard Surf 'n Turf smell of chlorine and rare meat was overpowered by whatever Tip-Top was processing. Usually the stench was burning plastic, a mechanical pungency that smelled like a computer printer in heat. On those days the grounds of Surf 'n Turf were empty except for the employees who wandered around with paper napkins stuffed up their noses.

The sharp edges of the desk began to soften like putty and Joe placed both feet on the ground, looking around the office. They could take the water-cooler, long-drained and useless, and the life-sized suit of armour which was given to him by an overseas investor. They could take anything in the piece-of-shit office except for the two fake diplomas which hung above the desk. He stood and took them off the wall while reading the printed Latin under his name. A B.Sc. in Chemistry and an MBA in International Relations.

For all he knew the Latin could be labelling him a first rate asshole. The ex who managed the printing of Pearlman degrees had been in the process of rigging him a Ph.D. when he broke up with her for Lulu. A Dr. of Exercise Science if he remembered correctly. Or, as he told her, a specialization in punching balls. Should have held out on that one, he thought. Dr. Pickles. It sounded like a high quality relish.

The Beige Years—that's what Lulu called the period before she met Joe. Chick was eight and they were living in a one-bedroom apartment above Bee-Bee's Butcher Shoppe. They only ate the beige-coloured food donated by a group of nosy nuns who ran a support group for pharmaceutical addicts in the basement of their church. Lulu did not have a pharmaceutical addiction but knew if she pretended, the nuns would give her boxes of food. Day-old bread, noodles with margarine, mealy potatoes, and boiled oats—when Chick got scurvy, Lulu tried to convince him it was a pirate disease.

The support group was led by an accountant named Hilda who'd overcome an addiction to Keen. She was an immaculate, well-dressed professional in her mid-fifties who approached every action with precise symmetry, whether it was the perfect circle of chairs she arranged at the beginning of each meeting, the placement of a Nanaimo bar in the exact centre of a paper plate at the refreshment table, or the well-timed rhythm with which she'd chew a piece of gum on each side of her jaw. As Hilda explained, she'd discovered that Keen stimulated an electric flare in her nerve endings that mysteriously simplified numerical values into shapes.

"Although terrifying," she told the group with a steady, clipped enunciation that reminded Lulu of a typewriter clacking, "it was a boon for my career. I didn't rely on a calculator anymore. All I needed was a pencil, a piece of paper, and a client's dossier. I've brought notes composed during the peak of my addiction." She passed a sheet of watermark paper around the circle. Lulu stared at the perfectly symmetrical diamonds, squares, triangles, and ovals drawn in pencil. It was like staring at the hieroglyphics of a computer language. She noticed that a few members of the group had begun to nod with understanding. She nodded a few times just to fit in.

"We're all here because we've experienced this exact dilemma," Hilda continued, placing the sheet of paper in her leather attaché. "Keen, Coda, Remark, and Tenet are just a few of the pharmaceuticals that increase our ability to work, think, and socialize. But let's not approach these meetings as a regression. Let's approach them as a return."

A light pattering of applause. Lulu quickly re-read the symptom guide she'd researched on Remark, her addiction of choice.

Positive

- easy cocktail banter
- performative/entertaining
- generous
- "life of the party"
- sexually voracious

Negative

- intolerance to alcohol (3:1 ratio per drink)
- "hammy" (e.g. Talk Show Host Syndrome)
- tendency to binge spend (most case studies indicate a propensity for purchases from 2:00—4:00am via home shopping networks)
- insomnia and sleepwalking
- sexually voracious

She should have made a grand gesture at the meeting, broken into a little song and dance and given everyone a foot massager or a set of knives that cut through bone. *Raise the razzmatazz*, she wrote next to the symptom guide.

At the refreshment table during the break, Joe sidled up to Lulu and cleared his throat.

"I'm using Desist," he whispered. She tapped whitener into a styrofoam cup of coffee.

"Desist?" she asked.

"Yeah, it's this new pill. Not on the market but works like a fucking dream." He absently reached for a miniature sugared donut. "Do you want some?" he offered casually.

"The donut or the pill?"

He looked at the donut for a moment, "Either, I guess."

"I'm ok on the donut. What does the pill do?"

"Curbs the craving."

"Do you take it orally?"

"You could." He paused for a moment and lowered his voice to an inaudible rasp. "I snort it."

"It's a word," she looked at his nametag, "Pickles. Desist is just a word. It doesn't mean anything. It's still a pharmaceutical."

Joe bristled and ate the donut, the powdered sugar forming a milky paste in the corner of his mouth. "I need a drink," he said.

"Me too." She set the coffee down on the table and they left.

Joe bought Vitamin C for Chick, a four-storey house with a microwave and a satellite dish, the top floor filled with old stock from failed infomercials—Orbitrek elliptical trainers, Scalpmed anti-hair loss pomade, and Ionic Breeze air purifiers which were yanked off the market after a few reports of bleeding lungs. Joe finagled Lulu a weathergirl job and put Chick in the only private school in Ransomville. But most importantly, Joe fronted the start-up for Lulu's Luau Lounge after Lulu was fired for miming a rainstorm. It was Joe who invested in the business and obtained the first storefront. It was Joe who taught her to take people's money like it was her right.

"Why else do we live in this fucking country," he'd repeatedly ask, "if we can't slash throats with dollar bills?" It was always about the cash cow, the cash crop, the cash out.

"In Toronto," Joe would say, "we literally ate shoestrings. Fucking shoestrings, boiled and salted like a plate of spaghetti." Many of Joe's statements about the past started with the words "in Toronto". Lulu had never been to Toronto and when she met Joe she imagined it to be a bombed-out wasteland with people scavenging in gutters. Since then she'd seen photos of Toronto—smiling white people in baseball caps ate lobster in the CN Tower's rotating restaurant; Chinatown bustled, the piles of fresh vegetables gleaming on the sidewalk stands; a toothy kid clutched a hot-dog in the Skydome bleachers. In all the photos, she hadn't seen the consumption of a single shoestring.

She could say it was sleeping on a lumpy mattress stuffed with wads of cash, or the Samurai swords in the corner of each room, or the daily doses of snorted Desist—the drug's pink powder smeared on every smooth surface in the house. But in reality, it was Surf 'n Turf. What started as a reckless vanity project soon became a maniacal fixation; all the winnings at the Hippodrome, the real estate in Ransomville, and any earnings on the slew of infomercial products were sunk into the business. Joe drifted in and out of their house like a stranger, rarely acknowledging Lulu or Chick. He would disappear for days, spending all of his time at Surf 'n Turf, sleeping upright in his office chair. When he did come home, it was for a change of clothes or to take a shower. He ate steak like salt; it was in everything. One time Lulu found him sprinkling finely chopped steak on a piece of steak.

"What are you doing?" she asked.

"Adding more flavour," he said gruffly.

"It's the same flavour, Joe. Steak flavour."

"Jesus Christ, Lulu. They're entirely different cuts," he yelled.

"Fine. I hope you get mad cow disease," she snapped.

He stopped sprinkling for a moment, "That's what I'm going to name the new waterslide. The Mad Cow."

The grounds were deserted except for one canteen attendee who absently flipped through a magazine.

"Are you closed?" Lulu asked the girl.

"Nope. Medium, rare, or deathly?" the girl responded automatically and inspected a cuticle.

"I don't want a steak. I just want to know where everyone is."

The girl bugged her eyes and sighed. "It's been pretty dead lately." She shrugged and flipped another page.

"Why are the waterslides still running?"

"Like I said, we're totally open," she paused and scrunched her nose, "except for the wave pools. Something's stuck in the wave making thingy."

"I'll take a Fluky then."

"Can I see some I.D.?" the girl asked. "Sorry, ever since that steak knife attack we have to ask everyone," she looked at Lulu up and down, "even people who are obviously way over."

Lulu flinched. She had an urge to smack this nasally pre-teen, with her everything-is-a-fucking-bore eye rolls. Relax, she told herself. She's just a kid.

"Forget it," she said.

She walked over to the wave pool to inspect. The chlorinated water was clouded with a reddish tint. There is a steak in there, she thought. No, a slab of raw beef; a severed cow limb. Something is bleeding unattended.

She found Joe in his office, asleep upright in his chair, the desk strewn with papers and pink powder. She cleared her throat like the sound of an engine about to stall.

"What's that?" he muttered, tugging his leather tie. He opened his eyes and looked at her. "What are you doing here?"

"I'm reporting you to the FDA," she said. "You're breeding e. coli, Joe,"

"In Toronto, e. coli ran through the streets like sewer overflow," he responded sleepily.

"I went to Toronto." She threw a manila envelope on the desk.

Joe brightened for a moment. "Really? Why?"

"For business. That city is as clean as a baby's asshole. But that's not why I'm here." She gestured at the envelope. "I'm suing you."

"What for?"

"Emotional duress, you shit." She leaned towards him and wrinkled the corner of her left eye. "See that? Each one of these creases symbolizes a year with you."

Joe nodded slowly and lit a half-stubbed cigarillo. "Too late," he said.

"What do you mean," she replied evenly.

"I'm already being sued," he said. "That Kellogg kid who was stabbed can only eat mushy food now. Some deep trauma brought on by the attack. You're too late," he repeated. "They're going to take everything."

"Everything?"

"Even these." He gestured at the steak-shaped paperweight shards on the ground.

Lulu chewed on the inside of her lip. A cow's head in the bed, a branded FUCK YOU on his shoulder—what would get through to him? Joe was not interested in nuance. He had the subtlety of a bag of potato chips.

After Lulu left, Joe walked up the concrete path to the top of the Mad Cow. His breath was short and jagged, a spike in his throat that pierced with each step. He lit a cigarillo and leaned against the chain link fence with what he hoped was a tough nonchalance. A few kids scampered past, the only he'd seen all day. He raised a hand and waved calmly.

"Just taking in the view, boys," he said and dragged on the cigarillo.

At the entrance to the waterslide, the kids shivered in wet swim trunks. The fog from Hint Hill had rolled in. Joe thought it looked like cotton batting—the insides of a stuffed animal split and strewn. The kids stepped lightly from foot to foot, their skinny arms crossed over their chests as they waited for their turn. Where was the lifeguard—that god-awful beluga schmuck with his inappropriate swim wear and slimy teeth? The first kid in line leapt into the waterslide, each arm pushing the sides of the chute to gain speed. A hoot echoed through the first tunnel, a tiny "woo woo" that sounded like the victory cry of a faraway sports fan. Joe slowly smoked the cigarillo and watched the rest of the kids get sucked into the slide. He looked at his watch. The grounds were officially closed so he'd have to give the lifeguard guff tomorrow.

All that water. He thought of the silos upon silos of water rushing through the system of chutes and tunnels opening on to the splash pools. He'd heard once that humans are half water but never believed it. People are drawn to themselves, to what they know. They should have been drawn to Surf 'n Turf. Nowhere else was there this much water. There was the wave pool, the adults' hot tubs, the wading area for toddlers who were below the 3 foot Mr. Turf cut-off. There were the wishing wells at the entrance, and the cattle fountains—an entire herd that stood upright on two legs and spouted streams of water. Joe swallowed with deliberation and felt a dryness in his mouth, as if his tongue had shrivelled into a prune. Someone has replaced my saliva with sand, he thought.

Try to remember the taste of Fluky, Freeze-Outs, Sipsy fountain drinks, he told himself. He closed his eyes and pictured a battalion of beverages engineered to relieve thirst. Thirst-Busters, a gang of animated soda pop cans who kick butt for hydration. They'd wear sunglasses and carry weapons of the musical theatre variety—baseball bats, chains, maybe a lead pipe or two. It was just the kernel of an idea, but he could run with it. He could come back. He poked a finger into his breast pocket and retrieved a lint ball. Why couldn't the world's tiniest water bottle have been tucked in there? The World's Tiniest Water Bottle, he thought again. It had a nice ring to it, kind of cutesy.

Joe lit another cigarillo and felt a shooting sharpness in his chest, as if a troupe of rusty nails were tap-dancing with frenetic indecision. The cigarillo dropped to the ground. The fog seemed to thicken. He steadied himself by grabbing on to the meaty shoulder of a Mr. Turf statue. Its smiling, senseless head lit up and drawled from a hidden speaker, "Ride on Pardner!" Joe gripped on to Mr. Turf and felt the fog move over him. It was like standing in a jar of smoke. He could no longer tell where his body ended and the fog began.

Jeff Miller

Workers' Entrance

Our boots tore black holes in the white skin covering the road. The snow fell so slowly that each flake appeared stitched to the sky. There were few streetlamps, but the glow of the city lit the night sky a soft pink.

The streetcar had left us on a bright corner. In both directions the street was lined with shuttered businesses and the doors leading to the apartments above them. We walked away from the light, under a train trestle and into an empty quarter.

We were travelling. We had spent hours on buses and in cars and were now approaching tonight's destination through wide empty streets, following the vague directions dictated to Rori over a pay phone.

I was seventeen and Rori was the presiding angel of my teen years. Eight years my senior and my best friend, he bore the burden of patiently bursting my bubble. He slowly talked me out of my awful ideas and shepherded me into other ways of seeing.

It was quiet and the streets were perfectly still. The snow accumulating in soft layers over everything made me think of the layers of dust that collected on the counters of my grandfather's basement workshop after his stroke.

This neighbourhood was once the workshop of the city. A giant shadow appeared on our horizon, a relic from those years. It grew larger with every step we took and in a few minutes we stood before it, examining its intricacies.

The factory was brick and climbed into the sky, dozens of stories high. Near the roof, the name of a vanished company was painted in white. The wind and years had stripped the words until all that remained were lines and shapes robbed of meaning. The windows were set in carved moldings and a cornice ran along the roof's ledge. We walked past a wide doorway fringed with delicate wood curlicues. The faded paint above it could still be read. Workers' Entrance.

"Workers' en*trance*," I said, deliberately mispronouncing it.

"When were these built?" I asked.

"Before the war. Or after," Rori said, not specifying which war.

"I wonder what they made here?"

"Probably something terrible." Where he was from there was a crayon factory. Throughout his childhood he imagined that inside the grey box on the edge of town there was a magical world of colour. When he was seventeen, his friend got a summer job at the plant. "It just sucked," he once told me. "At the end of the day she was covered in wax and colour. She had to scrub for an hour to get it off her skin."

"It's beautiful," he said of the factory in front of us. "But we wouldn't say that if it was still being used. Or if we had to work in it."

Consulting his directions, Rori led me past six more factories before we found the one Wil lived in.

"Do you guys want water? I've got water." Wil buzzed around us, gingerly stepping over our wet coats and bags, which lay in a pile near the front door. "Here, I'll get you some water." I watched Rori's friend as he let the taps run a moment, testing it with his finger to see if it was cold enough. I knew Wil was older than me but there was no hair on his face.

His loft was a nest. The windows were giant and the ceilings tall, but everything else was human sized. It wasn't much more than a loft-bed, a sink, a work table and the art on the walls. The bathroom, he told us, was down the hall. The bulletin board next to the table was covered with snapshots of young men. Years later a photo of me on an old high school ID card would be added to the board.

My water came in a mug with a chip out of the brim and a winking pirate gripping a knife in his teeth on the side. I was parched and drank so fast that I barely noticed that the tap water here tasted differently than at home. Rori sipped slowly; his mug was pink and populated by tiny ballerinas.

Wil turned his chair to face us, perched on it and, grabbing material from his work table, sewed as he talked. "What's up?" He watched us intently.

We told him our point of origin and our destination and the strange things that had already happened along the way. He nodded, saying 'oh' and 'really' and then added his own stories.

While still talking or listening, Wil sometimes put down his sewing to rummage through one of the clear garbage bags stowed beneath his table. They bulged with hundreds of pairs of used boys' underwear. Wil's art practice was transforming tighty-whities purchased at the Goodwill Buy-the-Pound store into a soft universe of art. He stretched quilts of undies over frames, sewed black and white Jolly Roger flags from them and hung them intact from half-empty wine bottles so they resembled the wicks of molotov cocktails.

His first solo show caused an uproar in the press for a few days. For months afterwards his answering machine message was a recording of an enraged talk radio host almost screaming the words "It's perverted! It's not art! *Boys' underwear*!!!???"

"What are you making?" I asked.

"I'm working on a nurse theme. My new boyfriend's HIV-positive so I figured it was a good fit."

He pulled a plastic container filled with his latest pieces from under the table. I sifted through the objects, each covered by a thin membrane of cotton. I picked up one that was long and narrow, unsure of what it was.

"Those are pieces from a Fisher-Price doctor kit."

I placed them on the floor and the shapes came into view. Stethoscope, reflex hammer, thermometer, blood pressure sleeve, all tightly wrapped in white.

In the hours that had passed since our arrival Rori had pulled the blanket sitting beside him over his legs. His thick stubble revealed that he had been up since dawn.

"How many people live here?"

"Just me."

"I mean in this building?" I asked. Rori was nearly asleep, but I never got tired when I was a teenager.

"Uh, a couple dozen. These are studios. We're not legally allowed to live here, but the landlord doesn't care."

"Is everyone here an artist?" It was a naive question, but I had never imagined these places existed, or even *could* exist.

"This is nothing. Just a few blocks from here there's this old warehouse that's something like a mile long. There's this subculture of people who never leave. They bike in there for exercise, live off welfare and get their groceries delivered."

"Let's go," I said. Rori woke at our prodding and groaned. He put his jacket on slowly and hated us.

Outside, the snowfall thickened until almost nothing before us was visible. Wil guided us through his familiar streets to the warehouse, its size impossible to discern in that squall. The first door we tried was unlocked. As we stepped inside, Wil told us a rumour that a sculptor with studio space here used a live baboon as a model.

"A baboon?"

"Well, some kind of monkey. But a big one, I'm pretty sure."

Apparently the creature had disappeared from its cage a few weeks back. No one had seen it since, but several people had said they felt as if something were watching them when they travelled the corridors late at night.

At first the warehouse was just a long narrow hallway. Wil unravelled tales of the artists, drug dealers, fashion designers and crusty punks that shared the space. We passed hundreds of doorways, their outlines visible in the dim light. Although they were all closed, Wil's stories promised that each one opened in on a mystery. This dark corridor resembled one of those places in children's books where infinite worlds co-exist, compressed into a collection of portals; all different, all open.

The corridor came to an end, widening into the complete vastness of the warehouse. I was amazed; the open space felt like an airplane hangar in size but it contained only two couches in an L shape sitting on a rug in its centre, and next to them a coffee table, floor lamp and a small television on a milk crate. Enormous skylights forty feet above and rimmed with snow peered down on this strange domestic scene.

"Jesus," Rori laughed. "I have enough trouble decorating my living room. If it was this big—"

We walked through the colossal chamber and into another corridor, one that seemed to grow tighter and dimmer the further we walked. Time stretched in the dark and Wil admitted he had lost his way. Our tired eyes caught movements in the nearby shadows. We suspected that every creak of the floorboards was made by the claws of the sculptor's escaped baboon. In paranoid whispers, we decided the beast had been stalking us since our arrival.

We escaped down a flight of stairs and through a wide doorway. Outside we laughed at our fear as soon as the cold winter air hit our lungs. The storm had passed but the fallen snow still softened the night. In the clear air we saw the enormity of the warehouse, stretching far out of sight in both directions. We watched the heavy clouds peel away from the horizon to reveal the hidden sky, a molten bar of rising sun illuminating it a soft pink. We smiled at the sight and then turned our backs, retreating along white streets to our temporary home and sleep.

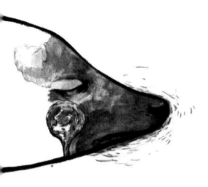

Vincent Tinguely

Set Up, Tear Down

I rode shotgun in a vintage green and white Dodge truck one summer. My friend Jackie was the driver and we were hauling a carnival ride, the Octopus, disassembled, wrapped in shabby canvas, roped and chained down so when it banged—and it did—it banged quietly. We stuck two or three joints into the mouth of a rubber dinosaur mounted on the dash, plugged a ghetto blaster into the dashboard lighter. Once Jackie got the rig up to highway speed and into fifth gear, I had to sit with my leg over the stick shift so it wouldn't suddenly pop out of gear. At one point I fashioned a forked stick to hold it in place, but less than an hour into that experiment the gear shift popped out and snapped the stick in half, so it was back to the old leg trick. I got used to sitting splayed out like that for hours at a time, as we made our circuitous way from one spot to the next.

We'd just torn down in Geraldton and were heading for Hornpayne, about 250 kilometres away. We got the thing up to cruising speed, one eye out the back window to make sure we weren't losing any of the ride's bits and pieces, and sparked one up. Hornpayne was in an unusual locale. I mean, Northern Ontario is almost by definition wild country, Shield country, humping scab-coloured rocks a billion years old, covered with a sprinkle of soil and topped with gnarled Tom Thomson pines. But along the highways there were almost always signs of human activity—sand pits, truck stops, junkyards, roadside tourist stands, trailer communities or pathetic attempts at farming. But once we turned onto Highway 631 there was literally nothing but bush. As we descended into a great, deep green pine-forested valley spreading itself out upon either side of the road, I thought Hornpayne was shaping up to be a beautiful spot, after the scrubby, sandy, littlesticks landscape of Geraldton.

You've got to have pride in your ride, Jackie always said. Which meant, no matter what you were running, even if it was a kiddie ride, you had to run it right. Make sure it was maintained. Not just maintained, but spruced up—touch up the paint job where it's chipped; grease the steel wheels under the buckets; if something's dangling, or bent, or frayed, fix it or replace it.

"That's easy for you to say, you run the biggest ride," Bear said. Bear ran the Whirly Bird, thought it stunk and said so to anyone who asked. I guess these guys were overly conscious of the bigger carnivals, the A and B circuits, with their gigantic rides—The Wild Mouse, the Zipper. I really didn't get it. A fugitive from university—this was my first and last summer as a carnie—I thought the ferris wheel I ran was 'big'. So did a lot of the rocking, rolling shitkickers who climbed aboard in Red Lake, Vermillion Bay, Fort Frances. "Stop rocking your seats!" I'd endlessly yell at these wasted bastards.

Jackie was talking about holding the line against sheer entropy. We were losers in the employ of a thoroughly fly-by-night C circuit carnival, working insane days, either setting up, tearing down or running rides from twelve to fourteen hours a day. Now we were in the process of closing a quiet, modern lounge in a brown brick shopping complex in 'downtown' Hornpayne—the complex itself constituted most of 'downtown' Hornpayne. Bear, an ex-hippie with a shaved head and a gorilla body was refusing to back down. "I'm not gonna have any fuckin' pride in my ride, if my ride fuckin' sucks!"

Our boss, Hoss, grabbed a chair and sat down, moving with a bouncy alacrity unusual for a man of his substantial girth. He slapped a sheaf of posters down on the beer-stained table. "So, is everybody ready to open tomorrow?" he said, mock-jovially.

"We're opening the day after," I said stupidly. I was half-dead with accumulated exhaustion. We'd been on the road for over a month, with not a day off. All my clothes stank, I stank, we all stank. Expecting a nice leisurely day ahead of us to set up the rides, Jackie, Stash, Yesh, Bear and I had just dropped acid. Hoss chortled.

"Well, *you* thought we were opening the day after, and *I* thought we were opening the day after, but the *printer* thought we were opening tomorrow." He unrolled one of the posters, which had been posted all around town for the past several days. Sure enough, the opening date was wrong. "So guess what?"

Bear reared up angrily. "I can't fuckin' believe it." He was the epitome of our collective disgust.

"Believe it," said Hoss. "We open at noon tomorrow!"

To make the noon opening deadline, we had to start setting up early in the morning. At three a.m. I was optimistically wrapping myself in a damp quilt in the front cab of another old truck. I hoped I was wrecked enough on cheap draft beer to counteract the crummy acid and allow me to pass out. I had to sleep curled up like a snail in its shell on the truck's narrow bench seat; this was the norm on set up or teardown nights when the steel-sided cargo trailer I usually crashed in was still stuffed to the brim with kiddie ride parts.

So we rolled out of bed at some insane, early hour. I felt like I hadn't even had a chance to close my eyes before they were being peeled open in a grey, grim, muggy morning. The minute I fell out of of the truck's cab I was being attacked by blackflies.

I ran the wheel but I didn't set it up. Mainly, because the wheel was the easiest ride of all to set up. It kind of unfurled from its trailer like a big Japanese fan and usually all I had to do was hook up all the lights, unfold the seats, top up the diesel engine and let her rip. All the 'big' rides used their trailers as platforms except for Jackie's ride, the Tilt-a-Whirl. So I was part of the Tilt crew, along with the rest of the 'big' guys—the curmudgeonly Bear; ex-biker Yesh; big Beef the joint mogul; Fred who blathered the summer away at his throw-the-ball-in-the-hole game; and Huey-of-the-dart-throw, who sported a major moustache and ignored me for the most part. Other than me and Fred, they all had 'staches, except Yesh who had a full-on beard.

Setting up the Tilt was insanely complicated, starting with the googly rail which of course went up and went down like waves, lovely woozley waves that encouraged riders to barf up undigested candy floss and pogos. This track had to be perfectly aligned by the expert, Jackie, who, having pride in his ride, would take forever to chock this up here, splint that there. To shove a board under something and twist the screwy things that the whole ride sat on. Fuck any of that up, and you'd have to disassemble the disastrous piece of shit and start all over again. It was more complicated than usual in Hornpayne, because we were setting up the midway on an uneven, grassy field, rather than on solid asphalt or gravel.

I was mumbling for coffee, Jackie was sucking at an early-morning Big Gulp sort of thing he found somewhere. He was at his worst. It turned out he was sick, just coming down with something which, on top of a major hangover, made Jackie a major drag to work under. He was never the best at containing his pain, he'd just take it out on the rest of us. "Come on, come on, what the fuck are you doing there?"

From the centre hub went the skeleton rails, each of which weighed a tonne. Two of us had to lurch and lug them from the trailer and hook them up. At one end these rails had little steel wheels that rode on the wobbly track we'd already set up. These rails had to be able to go around without jumping off the stupid track or we'd have to set up the centre hub again.

Set Up, Tear Down

Well, we spent six hours or so putting together intractable tinkertoy monstrosities, all the while being dive-bombed by deerflies which, when they landed, made off with a chunk of flesh. You'd *feel* them tearing it off. A quadrillion blackflies were getting into my hair, in my nostrils, ears and under my collar driving me nuts. Bug juice was just about worthless because I was sweating it all off hauling great honking rails and bull plates hither and yon. And by then it was pissing down rain, and my hangover was just starting to really kick in when we'd finished setting up and the boss told us there was no time to grab a lunch, or anything, because the public was already starting to show up.

And there they were, already a line a mile long was forming in the dribbling drizzle in front of the ferris wheel. My ears had been bit so many times by blackflies, they felt like somebody'd been beating me about the head with a stick. You couldn't have driven a Sherman tank through the hungover mess in my brain. Before I knew it I was running full rides—every seat on the ride taken.

It would take a couple of minutes to load the lugans up, then you ran the ride for a couple of minutes, and then you started unloading them again. Remembering always to balance the large ones off against similarly large ones on the other side, never mind if it insults them when you pick them out of the line, "You there, you get on next," because you don't want the ride to shake itself into pieces because of the weight imbalance. Match the skinny little kids three-to-a-bucket with more skinny little kids.

The kids are sweet, they're having the kind of fun a Northern Ontario kid ought to be having with a ferris wheel, big wide grins and "Wheeee!" It's the drunken full-grown shits I can do without, who get on and without fail start rocking their seats wildly, no matter how often I tell them to stop. So I would stop the wheel when they were eye-level to me and tell them, "You rock it again, you get off the ride." And they'd rock it again, unbelievably, so I'd stop the ride and tell them to get off.

"I'm not getting off," the leader of one particularly intractable gang of drunks said, sullenly. "The ride's not finished."

"The ride's finished for you because it's not going again until you get off."

Then, as they lumbered off the ramp one of them turned around and said, "We'll get you, boy!"

Great… that's all I needed was some blackhead-stricken townie who weighed twice as much as me coming back for his luganish revenge. But I quickly forgot about them because there were another million maniacs to get into the wheel. Oh, Hoss must've been happy, we were making a fortune for him there in the grey greasy drizzle with the dancing little blackflies gnawing away at my neck, scalp, etcetera. As it turned out the drunks never made good their promise of revenge. Just my being in Hornpayne was enough revenge for them, I should think. I needed to shit. I needed to piss so bad my teeth were floating. I needed something to eat but I was so sick hungover I could barely stand the idea of eating, but still, I felt weak. Jackie put one of my tapes on the carnival sound system and so Hornpayne was being treated to *I Just Don't Know What To Do With My Life* by the Buzzcocks. I took fifteen seconds between rides to run over to the Tilt to yell at Jackie, "Perfect!!"

Fortunately for me, the rain got heavy, the crowds disappeared and we closed down. I lumbered soggily over to Jackie and said, "There's only one thing we can do in this situation."

"Which is?"

"Get a hotel room."

A hotel room was everything we missed about 'civilization'. Hot water, clean towels, cable television. So we booked into a room in the same downtown complex as the lounge. We showered, ordered a couple of large pizzas and crashed in front of the tube where we caught the last half of the *M*A*S*H* movie, an episode of *BJ and the Bear*, and some show on the Cable Health Network where a couple of prim-looking women engaged in an animated discussion about penises, orgasms and the like.

Next day I was sick, with a sore throat and general aches and pains. The wheel had been positioned on a slight rise overlooking the rest of the midway. A stand of shimmering beech and birch trees stood just in back of me. The blue sky of morning promised a full day of work. I didn't really care. I unfolded and wiped down the seats, topped up the fuel tank, and turned over the diesel. We opened at eleven in the morning and ran until eleven at night.

I passed in and out of a Zen zone, assuming everyone getting on the ride was't going to be an asshole, but was going to be a reasonable human being like myself. I put that out there for a while. It worked, until the drunks started showing up at dusk and then it was, "Stop rocking your seats!" time after time. Nothing ever got quite as ugly and threatening as the day before though. "Don't these pricks have lives?" I asked myself, throttling the ride down as I brought the latest load of lugans in for a landing.

Of course they didn't, not any more than I did. What exactly did we think we were doing, bashing this load of ridiculous whirling junk through Northern Ontario? It was well beyond the usual neo-colonial exploitation of logging and mining and suchlike. It was in a class by itself, a 'service' to the insanely bored denizens of these one-horse shitholes where everything revolved around a mine or a mill or maybe nothing at all. In Hornpayne it seemed to be nothing at all. I couldn't figure it out at any rate. It was in a beautiful pine valley and I hated it like poison because I was sick and tired and covered in welts from the blackflies. I hated it because we were playing Trooper, Teaze and Toronto, Triumph and all kinds of godawful shit until Jackie finally put on the Velvet Underground. Nobody noticed any difference. People were generally oblivious of anything beyond the rides. The rides, the rides, the rides. There was Jackie sluicing down yet another little 'accident'. "I'll never eat another pogo as long as I live," I swore to myself.

During the day the sun was out just long enough to make me wish it was still raining, the heat and humidity sending the blackflies humming in a mist around my swollen skull. Load 'em up. Let 'em ride. Throw 'em out, start a new load and do it again. It all went around and around like the wheel, and then all the lights were twinkling, it was dusk already. A patch of rain let us run off for a quick bite but then it was back at it until eleven, running the goddamn wheel for twelve straight hours. I was starting to go cross-eyed with exhaustion. Another bastard was swinging his seat. I hauled back the control shift and threw him off. I emptied the wheel, crossed the sward to Jackie and said, "I'm not running my ride any more!" But the lot was already empty, everybody'd gone home and we shut down for the night.

We walked across Hornpayne underneath a Wagnerian sky, every star shining like a hole punched through a black tin to let glory itself shine through. We were at the lounge again and the band's last set was cooking and I was liking it even though Bear and his Fu Manchu moustache thought the guitarist 'sucked'. "Compared to what?" I asked. "We're in fucking Hornpayne!"

Hoss invited everyone up to his hotel room to party after the lounge closed down, and so I found myself at one end of the room sucking back triples of rye, while he was hamming it up with some of the cover band musicians at the other end. I was distracted—it was impossible to 'be there' in my state of sheer exhaustion, shitfaced, so I gave up on trying to engage in any sort of conversation. What was the point of this, partying at three in the morning, sick as a dog, with another day on the midway to look forward to? We were just a gang of drunken apes, our only mission to turn the wheel, turn the wheel, turn the wheel. I was staring in a daze through a big window's half-turned venetian blinds at the blackness of the rail switching yard out there, the glimmer of tracks in darkness—suddenly there was a commotion at the other end of the room. Hoss had lost it, all three hundred pounds of him so hammered he'd started to randomly bash people. Various carnies were trying to calm him down, hanging off his thrashing arms like hounds worrying a grizzly at bay. I got one good look at his face, staring blindly—like my own dead, blind grandfather—through smoky lenses, his red Odin's beard pointing skyward as his great ham-like fists flew out, and one of them randomly connecting with Yesh's concerned-looking face. Poor old Yesh, who was only trying to help.

Next thing I knew I was outta there, back to the lot. I managed to blow up my air mattress in the empty kiddie ride trailer before I had to stagger outside and puke. Oblivion had once again been successfully solicited.

Hormone, one of the teenage gunsels who ran the kiddie

rides and shared the trailer with me, banged on its metal side at 10:30 that morning to rouse me. I cursed him. "Well you said to get you up," he said thickly. This was true. I had to get my overstuffed bag of stinking laundry done, get some mail sent, get a decent lunch into me. There'd be no other free time to do it before we had to leave town.

The show was over at six that day. We all straggled back to the lot in a fine drizzle of warm rain for tear-down, which, with the Tilt-a-Whirl, was just about as gruelling as set-up. Hauling plates and rails back to the trailer where Jackie supervised the stowage of everything. He winched the buckets up one by one. Everything had to be in its place, squared away, chained down. We finished up near midnight, and normally all the restaurants would've been closed by then, but Hoss had arranged for the local truck stop out near the highway to stay open just for us. What a dump it was, thrown together with plywood and sheet metal, a long counter with weary carnies ranged all along it on wobbly stools. We were served some sort of weird spaghetti and turkey loaf leftover mess, which at least was hot, and by Northern Ontario standards not too pricey.

The next morning, Jackie and I felt slightly more human by the time we were back in the cab of the green and white Dodge, driving to Terrace Bay. We were getting over whatever bug we'd picked up. Terrace Bay turned out to be a town completely unlike Hornpayne. There were no bugs, no drunks, and it was neat as a pin. I could find nothing wrong with it except for the stench of the pulp mill, but you could get used to that pretty fast. It was unlike Hornpayne in every way but one—we'd have to set up yet again.

Dan Gillean

Tightrope

It takes me some time to figure it out, but pretty soon I've reached the top of the telephone pole outside my apartment. It's six a.m. Everywhere, buses are heaving down the snowy corridors winter makes of the boulevards, taxis lining up in rows on busy corners. Beds are being made, rolled over in, alarms turned off or ignored; bodies dressing or dreaming, entangling themselves in each other a moment longer, as the sun gilds the first row-houses. The city shakes off its darkness everywhere, and I am stretching my foot out tentatively toward you. It's a long walk, but I'm not worried.

Tightrope

From up here, the city is almost orderly—streets gridding out the neighbourhood, the demure parks fenced in by concrete. Telephone lines, power lines, cable cords and converters mirror the pipes and subways below, the alleys and avenues. The line from my apartment to your new condo, mapped in a geometry of wires.

If I look hard enough, I can almost see where the money runs in this city. Eight streets west of here the buildings become uniform and modern, the streets smooth and flat, the wires hidden. The unit your father bought you stands on the divide, like a gatekeeper to a world where I'm not welcome, an eddy line drawn where the cash flow cuts back on itself. Somewhere in the capital, in a neighbourhood just like this, your father is sleeping in a sparse and modern bed, his moustache twitching, buoyed by dreams of dollars as he floats peacefully through the night, toes dragging in the current. He sends a cheque to you every month, and a photograph once a year.

Around me, the wind curls whorls of snow off the roof-tops, and the day begins to colour. I've got to hurry.

The thing about a tightrope is the attention it demands. A brooding paramour, it brooks no suitors waiting in the wings, no half-hearted struts and steps. Only pure dedication. But I am not single-minded enough as I step out; already I'm thinking of the descent, your face framed by the kitchen window, the telephone resting on the counter. My foot slips from the telephone wire, and I'm stumbling, the street spinning sickeningly below. One foot swinging, I lean back into the pole, feel the hard smack of the wood, the smell of pitch and electricity circling in my nostrils. Beneath my feet, I can feel the click of a call connecting, pulsing down the line:

Hello? Steven, are you up yet?
I'm up, I'm up.

It's Mrs. Lampman in the apartment downstairs, calling her son, making sure he doesn't cut another class. I take a deep breath and look down the line. Focus.

Pretty soon I'm doing it, toes curled around the insulating rubber, scissoring my feet, arms extended. It's slow going. I can feel the wires singing, a steady stream of talk shivering up my legs, buzzing out my fingers, fluttering around my ears like so many moths. I make it out over the alley, where there's nothing to hold onto but faith. Snippets of conversation, shipment details, automated messages—*Jerry are you going to … Welcome to ExTerra's automated … Fuck you … The time now is … Hello Please enter your … Not if I see you first.*

Concentrate. When my mind starts to wander, down the line toward you, or back to the mess in my apartment, the wire begins to sag and groan beneath me. I shake and tremble on the thin strip of black mapping my route, breathe, and measure my steps to you.

I think about the words. What I might say if this were a phone call instead of an impossible circus act. I hear that you're knee deep in women now, and it's hard not to laugh at that—but I don't want to be petty. It's been more than six months since we've spoken, and there's so much I could tell you about—should I tell you I've stopped seeing Dr. Palmer, or that I came out to my parents and my mother won't speak to me? That my brother hit an IED outside Kabul and might never wake up? That I quit my job?

After the first month, you had my number blocked, your father's idea no doubt. I can feel all that frustration, all those unsaid words, rising in me. But as I think these things, my feet begin slipping, and the moths surge and swarm around me, my arms pinwheeling in the open air.

Tightrope

I gasp and stumble, wobble and shake on my wire, as the pavement below warps and rises, filling my vision. Somehow, bending my knees, my arms planed out, I manage to stay up. Eyes pinched shut, I draw a jagged breath, feel the moths tickling my skin. Keep breathing. I don't know what would happen if I fell now, but it couldn't really be worse than what's behind. The wind licks my skin; tiny grains of airborne ice bite my fingers, cheeks, and toes. The moths crowd my ears with their talk. A tightrope leaves no room for distraction. I need something to hold onto.

It comes to me then—our last trip together, before your father found us out, canoeing on the river near my parents' cabin. We began arguing about something, the details forgotten now, and I stood as our voices rose. Soon you were on your feet too, and the canoe rocked wildly as we pointed and shouted, until the weight of our anger reached its tipping point, and I tumbled over the side. You laughed, your face shedding its furrows, and then jumped in with me. We clung to the side of the canoe, shivering together, chuckling as we kicked toward shore.

That moment—your smile cresting, twisting the pout from your lips, eyebrows unknitting as I sputtered and surfaced, the anger gone as you stripped off your jacket, your shirt, your boyish muscles gleaming in the sun. Sometimes the only way back to balance is to tumble over the tipping point.

I cup that moment in my palms now, a hard, bright gem against the blank void of the sky above me. Something solid and brilliant to cling to—a counterweight to stabilize me as I walk. My feet steady on the wire as the words come to me. I wanted you there, poised to jump out of that canoe forever, but I don't blame you for turning your back on that world, choosing security, approval, over the cold cut of the water. Your father's an important man in the capital. And beneath that skein of sun and muscle, you were also something small and blinking in the light. But I know why I'm up here now, what it is I need to tell you. I grip that ruby instant and stretch my foot out once more. The line becomes taut again, and I'm walking quickly now, crossing the street, skipping around a pole, moving closer. Back at my apartment, someone's knocking on the door, and I've got to go faster.

I'm running now, it's easy, it's urgent, and I'm crossing blocks at a time, the space between my steps widening, until I can feel it overhead—the tangled network of cell phone transmissions, thickening as the day breaks. Time's important now, so I grab a hold of a thin stream of conversation, a construction worker talking to his boss:

Larry make sure you get those casings done this morning, you want anything in your coffee?

Nah, See you soon.

And then the line is pulling apart, but already my feet are on the next one, and I'm running and climbing through the air, spinning out over the streets, higher and higher. The city is shrinking beneath me, the air cooling as I rise, and I'm looking for your street, your building, your window. Only soon, I can't make sense of the mess up here, and the moths are swarming around me, languages clashing together, darting apart. There's not enough order to this jumble, webs instead of wires, and the moths are in my face, my hair, filling my mouth until I stumble and drift loose on the wind. I see the steeple of a church rise up towards me and throw myself towards it, letting the lines go, hitting the peak hard, knocking the swarm from me. Hands shaking,

I grip the panelled roof and try to catch my breath. Better stick to simpler geometries.

It takes me twenty minutes to get back to a pole. My feet are freezing. I've drifted too far south and have to turn back, stumbling when I think too much. I'll be too late if I don't hurry. It's harder to travel in your new neighbourhood, where they keep the wires out of sight, but I manage. I'm running along my tightrope now, I've got it, my mind focused, and your street is coming up, full with the morning commute trundling below me as I cross. I can see your window now. There you are, just as I imagined, sipping a coffee, a robe pulled tight around your shoulders, the phone beside you. The words gel themselves inside my mind—more than anything, I need you to know that this, now, is not about you. I should have made that clear, and now I'm racing to make it count, before it's too late.

Only the telephone is ringing, and I'm yelling at you not to answer it, but your finger is on the talk button, the call surging beneath me, and before I can get there you turn away, cocking your head to listen.

Mr. DiBlanca, this is the police, do you know a Mr. David Schultz?

Well, yes, what is it?

You were listed as his emergency contact number?

But that's crazy we haven't spoken in—wait, emergency?

I'm too late. The ruby gripped in my palm is suddenly warm and wet, dripping a trail of red in the snow. You're taking it in as I cross the last stretch, pressing my face to the window—you're sweeping your breakfast from the table, wondering what I used to make the cuts, stamping your feet until the neighbours below begin knocking on the roof, hanging up the phone and throwing it against the wall. What good are wires now. You sit and sob. On the floor, a cheque and a photograph covered in egg. In any act of balance, there is a tipping point. The thought comes to you, I can see it—it's a joke, some cruel form of revenge, and I watch the brief surge of hope flicker across your face, your mouth pulling tight at the corners as you begin to rise. For a moment you pause, standing now, hesitating by the window—one foot raised on the edge of the canoe, waiting for me to surface. You pick up the phone and call me, the number still memorized, hoping someone will answer, but I'm not there.

Wasela Hiyate

Jeanne Mance Park

The air is still, with the faint smell of garbage hanging like a balloon outside your window after circling up the fire escape. But you've gotten used to this recurring Wednesday odour. When you first arrived, you had your choice of rooms. Sandra sashayed about like a madam pulling open door number 1, the yellow room with the large window that opened onto l'Esplanade, then number 2, the larger, dimmer room with a window that overlooked the deep well of the fire escape. You thought it was a private, peaceful space, separated from the other adjoined bedrooms, though you couldn't have anticipated the smell. The view of the brick wall made you laugh, made you choose this room. You know you got it because of the way you look: no chance of you being mistaken for Québécois *pure laine*, more like an Amazon Filipina with your father's height, your mother's hair. More exotic since the referendum. Your skin is some shade between black and Chinese, though in summer you darken and your mother gives you a jar of beauty cream, the same kind your cousins use, skin bleach.

Clack-click. Even when she's barefoot from the shower, you can identify Sandra just from the strike of her heels. Moira's tomboy shoes have no urgency in their tread: she makes no demand for attention. The sensible eighty-percent absentness of her only takes up the space of her bedroom. You open your door and there stands Sandra, stark naked in golden strapped shoes in the living room, putting up her hair for tonight's show in front of a mirrored wall. Of course her carefully bound platinum locks will be wildly tumbled after this evening's performance, depending especially on how many laps she'll ride after dancing with the pole. She toys with the CD player that sits on the piano and returns to her reflection, sings with a Horace Andy tune as she practices putting in a hairclip, pulling it out. She watches how the hair falls and whether it spills just so. Her hips swerve to the smooth reggae beat. She hasn't returned the filmy white blouse she spied in your closet weeks ago, but why should you worry, at least someone's making use of it.

"Lucy, I'm wearing your top again tonight." She smiles at your reflection in the mirrored wall, as if reading your thoughts. "All the guys love it. You don't mind if I keep it for a bit longer?"

"Don't worry, I'll take it back when I need it." Though you doubt you'll ever need it again.

The buzzer sounds. You answer the door for Jean-Paul who always gives you a sweet smile and asks: "*Sandra est lá?*"

"*Oui, mais elle est complètement nue.*" You wonder if there's a word for naked, the way nude and naked are different in English.

He laughs. "*Ah oui, c'est comme je l'aime,*" and his grin turns mischievous. Of course that's how he likes her. Jean-Paul saunters into the room with his practiced gait, cool and unhurried. They'd danced together in school. Sometimes you hear music blasting from her room, the door open and the two of them breaking, going over different steps, freestyling. That's why she went to school—dancing. This is obvious by the change you see if the right music's on, her essence focused on the movements of her body, her unguarded expression of rapture.

Uncanny that stripping entered her life at the same time pimping did his. She told you it was something like a family business, that his cousin asked him to be a partner in the venture. And no, she's never been one of his girls. "They're all Haitian anyway, like him. He takes care of them on the streets and he never sleeps with them. Christ, he doesn't call them *les soeurs* for nothing." When you're walking back from Foufounes Electrique and get to the corner of St. Laurent and St. Catherine, it's hard not to look at the faces—just to see if maybe Jean-Paul is out with his girls tonight, all of them sipping coffees in the corner Burger King.

The escapes to Parc Mont Royal are what you need after class, the | ...Your room with a view

easiest place to mix with Concordia and McGill artsies with their goatees and retro sneakers, jocks with their polo shirts holding beer cans, Université de Montréal and UQAM French boys in round spectacles, CEGEP hippies, assorted shirtless soccer players, drunkards, stoners, musicians and rastas. You're there after the final exam with some of the people in your design history class debating the pros and cons of the craft movement, one of the questions on the exam. Most of them are graduating, like you. Most of them are moving away where there won't be any language or cultural issues involved in getting a job somewhere in the field.

Funny how you got into art history, that high school teacher who stopped you on the staircase while you marched up to homeroom.

"You got the highest mark in the art history component. I don't know how, I guess you just have a high level of basic human intelligence." You wondered what kind of intelligence others had.

You remember her shock. Not that everyone knew your blackness. People guessed only because of the friends you hung out with, who never pushed themselves out of the tiny place of people's expectations for them. "Rudegirl is half Chiney," they'd said about you when you made the honour roll. "As long as the bottom half is black," said your boyfriend, squeezing your behind. The guidance counsellor in junior school had no idea what to do with you, felt you'd be happier with your friends in a technical school but suggested a collegiate anyway. And this is how your life has worked—on a dare.

You artfully smoke the *Gauloises Blondes* cigarette you bummed from the "it girl" of the class, an aesthete whose father is a successful New York artist. She's Chinese, like your mother, but she's a Wong and direct from China, not via the West Indies. She's no piece of *chinoiserie*. The boys are flirty, hoping to have a chance with her before leaving town, but she's playing it cool. You admire that about beautiful women. They know something about their worth and how to play the auction floor to their advantage.

The sun's going down and although you should be relieved, instead you're anxious. You haven't decided to leave the city. You're not sure what you want but you've been sketching a lot of studies, even drawing comics. What you're learning through practice: perspective is everything.

The fact that a few of your cartoons have been printed in the school paper is enough to encourage you. You'd like to print your own zine, but don't know how to begin. Maybe if you were the "it girl", things would be different. But you're sick of your own excuses, flick your cigarette into the grass. At least you know you aced that exam. You wrote about Turner because you loved that he painted British Parliament burning in the brilliance of gold, like the kind excavated from colonies in Africa and Asia, though this particular thought didn't appear in your essay. You wrote about his Slave Ship: its hellfire sky, its dirty sea of dead and sickly bodies that most of us have crossed in order to get here.

As the gang disperses, people confirm a pub-crawl happening on Saturday night. You look up to the window of your flat, just across the street. Your apartment swells with Sandra.

Pushing the door open, you're relieved to find that she's not there, only Moira tapping away at the typewriter, paid to write another one of Sandra's assignments. A furtive glance and stiff smile, Moira checking that you're not Sandra, then her friendly grin and "Helloooo" drawled from across the corridor. You run a bath, filled with lavender foam and images of the party last night. Moira's shoes step into your thoughts as she opens the front door and turns the lock when she's on the other side. She's meeting her girlfriend at work. The apartment is all yours.

You've barely slipped into clothes when you hear knocking at the door—three quick business-like raps. "*J'arrive*," you call out from your bedroom, knowing already that it must be for Sandra: a musician, a DJ, a pimp, a dealer, a music biz type. Sometimes they speak English but are uncomfortable using it. But some of them, used to plying girls with words in any language that might communicate a way into their beds, are very skilled with English. You open the door and find a face you remember from a picture Sandra keeps on her dresser. He's waiting patiently on the landing, in a drastically different mood from his knock, with a beautiful smile and longer dreads than he has in the photo. It's her ex, the one that she talked about incessantly when you first moved in, who'd been away on tour with his group. "*Est-ce que Sandra est là?*"

You tell him that she isn't at home but he's already wandered in and makes himself comfortable at the piano, his fingers finding a tune with ease as he asks if he could wait for her. You admit that you've no idea when she'll return. He just nods and smiles, plays something that's sad and familiar although you'd never be able to name it.

There's a clamour of feet on the staircase—the slow steady pace of heavy clogs stamping up behind the first pair. Jean-Paul steps through the door and stops dead when he sees someone sitting at the piano, then Sandra comes in and gasps, recognizing Ousman in mid-melody. He stops playing, grins at her, stands up.

"*Mais qu-est-ce que tu fais ici?*" Sandra gushes as she glides toward him. They hold each other in a long and warm embrace that makes Jean-Paul shift on his feet, cough. Soon both men are sitting on the couch with Sandra in the middle. So it's true, as she once told you: once you go black you don't go back. You make an exit to the kitchen, put together a *croque-monsieur* and sit down at the table. There's a hush in the next room as Sandra joins you. Opening the fridge door, she gives you an ecstatic look. "I can't believe he's here! Doesn't he look good?"

"Did you see how Jean-Paul looks?"

"You know what men are like," she frowns, pulling your last big bottle of *Maudite* from the fridge. "I'll get you back." She minces into the living room with an arm full of glass tumblers.

You know what men are like. As you became more involved in your courses, the boys changed too. You needed bookish, artistic men, though there were fewer each year. And, for some reason, your romances are shorter than they used to be. Now the boys you choose are all pretty, with light, startled eyes, as if to concede to your Aunt's request, "when you going to bring home a blue-eyed boy?"

The last one you took back to your place after a concert. You asked him to tie you up the morning after. He was surprised, intimidated. You showed him how to make the knots in the scarves. He did as you asked. His cock stood up in his shorts, made you wet.

"Hit me," you said.

"What?"

"Hit me."

He kissed you instead, untied your legs to sting you with a good spanking. His slaps travelled up your body. It felt so good you were almost smiling. For some, it's just the mix of sensation they like. For you, the warmth of love has always been delivered by a strong hand. His smacks became harder. You moaned. His face changed to pleasure, then surprise; he didn't know how much he'd enjoy this. His eyes glittered darkly. You were telling him not so hard when he laid into you with a punch that winded you and then he slapped you and your face got whipped the other way, so you were staring at the Hundertwasser poster on the wall. You'd never tasted fear like that. You swallowed it—forced yourself to breathe. Your neck felt funny and you wondered if you were paralysed, but your feet had already kicked him off. Your hands frantically untied the knot designed for emergency escape. "What's wrong, didn't you like that?" He came at you again. You got your other hand out in time and struggled with his sweaty weight, pushed him off. He panted, surprised by your fight. He stepped back, smirking, took a cigarette from a pack on your dresser, lit it as you shook, swollen, your body throbbing. You felt the warm wetness at the corner of your mouth, tasted the blood. He leaned against the dresser, smiled at you. You grabbed his pants and took out his wallet. The smirk fell off his face. The pants flew towards him and you threw the wallet out the window, heard its padded landing onto a plastic bag. "You better get it. I think it's garbage day," you said, steel-voiced.

He glared at you, pulled on his pants. He flung open the door, stormed through it. You grabbed your robe and locked all the doors as he shouted threats back up the stairs.

You didn't leave your room that day, or the next. You lay there, one of the bonds still around your wrist, remembered the way you were drunk at that party and couldn't stop looking at The Roots CD insert: the ship hull layout of black bodies manacled, the space designed to carry as many people as possible. The diagram never appeared in any history book you ever went through and you wondered why, though you know the power of an image.

They knocked on your door, asked if you were alright. When they saw you again, you could explain the swelling. It was good to be outside, to feel the sun. The bruises faded under the darkness of your skin.

Throughout your lunch you hear Sandra's titters and Ousman's excited chatter about his newly released Zoukous CD, the one spinning music throughout the apartment. You hear Jean-Paul's sullen silence, the beer being drunk, a joint passed around. The tension of the apartment seems like the perfect reason to get some air on the mountain. You'll take your sketchbook, do some drawing in the green hills and yellow trees that will soon be covered in snow and ice.

Walking up the sloping path where your favourite park bench waits, you can't help smiling at the hikers, bikers, joggers, couples, dog-walkers and students exploring the hilly landscape. Up on the mountain, it feels as if the entire city revolves around you. The west neighbourhoods, mainly English, the east neighbourhoods, mainly French, then the mix of south and north. You follow the ever-winding asphalt path to the top and take in the view of the downtown from the lookout. Everybody points at the buildings shaped like huge cocks, though they're not always sure what compels them to point. You walk around the semicircular platform, take in the view of the entire downtown area while you puff on your Matinee Lights, study the Lachine Canal, the Old Port and the liquid clouds of the blue sky.

This is where he starts talking to you, the lanky guy with thick black curls. He digs into his knapsack and pulls out a bottle of water.

"Where are you from?" he asks with a slight Québécois accent.

You'd spied him on the mountain path; he seemed to be drinking in the view on the walk up, slowly, serenely. There was a camera slung around his neck, but he didn't have the same lost-in-adventure look that tourists had. The friendly way he asks the question disarms you. "It's a long story." You give him the short version of Caribbean history: sugar, slaves, migrant workers, independence, problems.

"I guess we're both a little mixed up," he laughs, confesses his native-French background. "Us Québécois, we're the white niggers of North America."

You're about to roll your eyes when you see the twinkle in his. Irony. Good.

Soon, you are both engaged in a dizzying conversation as you find the path winding down the mountain. The setting sun bathes the park in golden light and you skip over your lengthening shadows, talking about the warring sides of your family. Maxim tells his own story of genesis, native and French, members of his family in denial of the native blood in them. Then the unending arguments since the referendum last year, about the immigrant population of Montréal ruining everything. He picks up a dried leaf, marbling orange and crimson from green already and sighs deeply, as if exhaling the world. "So much trouble. We forget to notice the beautiful, the astonishing."

You realize it's why you draw. Your eyes narrow on him, he looks away self-consciously, pointing and laughing at a t-shirted dog doing tricks in the park.

By the second meeting you both have your cameras and scour the Park Avenue strip for flashes of inspiration: the right car colour combinations speeding by, the blur of faces of people moving on the grassy slopes, the late blooms among the withering and gnarled summer flowers, everything slowly dying. As the afternoon progresses, there is the developing appetite that makes you want to know everything about each other. Something in the back of your mind keeps telling you to stop, that there is plenty of time. But you want this impulsively, irrationally. Its sweetness is already making you drunk.

On a rainy afternoon you and Moira hang your heads out the window of the stuffy apartment, looking out at the park while sucking on a water bong, exhaling into the dark damp air. You're still in your pyjamas at 3:00 in the afternoon. She's in her tank and briefs. She's supposed to be writing essays, you're supposed to be thinking of your future. She tells you about Genevieve and soon you're both giggling like high school girls. "Montréal women have such attitude," she laughs. "It's strange, the English say 'I'm coming', the Japanese say 'I'm going' and you know what the French say?

"*Quoi?*"

"I'm here."

"No wonder we can't get along—we're always missing each other."

Moira suggests that you spend more time at Maxim's rather than suffer episodes with Sandra around, "because, you know," she moves her finger in a circle at the side of her head. You both laugh raucously, but you wonder if you're not getting it because you're high.

The next afternoon is rainy and mild. When you look out the window you see the neighbourhood kids playing frantically because they know the air, the heat of a Montréal summer that leaves just as you begin to thaw. You meet Maxim at a *casse-croûte* on Rachel Street. It's agreed that you'll both have your pictures developed. He's late and looks apologetic with his skewed-to-one-side smile. He digs into his canvas bag for the package of pictures.

"You haven't peeked at yours, have you?" you ask him suspiciously.

"Well, I tried not to, but I had to develop them," he says, matter-of-fact.

You cut your eye at him. He looks at you and his smile travels across his lips like a car running the curve of the mountain. His laughter evens out his face.

Intoxicated by the smell of coffee, toasted bagels, lox, eggs, sausage, and homefries, you both take in the view of the wet sidewalks. You watch the rain falling on umbrella tops, people's faces buried in their hoods as they hurry along the street, children running in rubber boots, and rain-glazed cars with windshield wipers scraping. You are part of a conspiracy that anyone else could join if they would just look up.

The wet afternoon expands into the evening. You're both sipping wine behind the glass of a St. Denis bistro. He talks about his martial arts teacher who spoke the Upanishads and Lao Tzu fluently during practice. "On the first day in the dojo, you know what we did?"

"What?" You're tickled by what sounds like a sexy story coming up.

"We just stood there."

"Like, side by side?"

"No. Facing each other. Two people standing, not moving, not talking, just breathing."

"Whoa."

"Yeah, it was intense. I lasted a minute. But the next time we stood there for ten." He tells you that it was all about learning to listen, which requires stillness. You cannot engage properly with an opponent, or, for that matter, a lover, until you've understood the violence within yourself.

...The man with the one way smile

You know as the two of you pass the *friperies* full of vintage clothing on Mont-Royal that you are slowly strolling to your building. When you're about to get to your front door, you ask him if he'd like to come in, to see the view of the park from the front room of the apartment. He is happily surprised by the invitation.

The next morning, you emerge from your room to find Sandra in baby dolls in the kitchen, alone, ashing a cigarette. She turns a distraught face towards you and you notice the smudged eye make-up, making her look like a drama queen from a soap opera. She tries to smile but you're instinctively careful about the cheeriness of your "good morning".

"Someone had a good night," she suggests. "I could hear you from across the hall, you know."

You smile, wondering what she could mean, since you talked most of the night, slept early in the morning. Though you knew you could trust him, you told him he might be more comfortable if he left. He graciously offered to sleep on the couch, could see your naked fear. But it strikes you as odd that your voices in conversation could travel quite that far. You help yourself to a cigarette from the package in front of her on the table.

"You know, next time you might want to turn up the music a little." She winks, flicking her lighter in front of your cigarette.

"Next time." You rub her back in appeasement. When you look down you see raised welts on her arms, some almost bleeding.

"What happened there?" you point.

"Nothing. I do that in my sleep sometimes." She waves it off as if it were nothing more than a pesky insect, though you've never noticed marks on her in the few months you've lived there.

On Sunday you and Moira enjoy an afternoon ice cream on Avenue du Parc, strolling toward the stone monument of the two lions, the rhythm of the tam tam drums already pounding through to your heart. Throngs of people dance and clap to the beat. Moira tells you about Sandra's mother who left her husband in New Brunswick for a happier life in Montréal. "You've probably seen her if you go to Club Monde. She's there every weekend, all dressed up, the older lady who can really dance."

You're both weaving through the crowds of people, perusing the vendors' wares of beaded handicrafts, clothing, pipes and hemp purses. There are girls braiding ribbon into people's hair and a henna artist. Some of the younger kids are sitting around a guitar player who's barely audible in the midst of the pounding drums. A bare-chested man with salmon pink skin and an iguana on his shoulder walks past you toward the steps where the drummers sit.

"When I started hanging out with Sandra she was happier. Then she wanted stardom, not just decent singing or dancing gigs. This all happened after Ousman left. He never asked her to go with him. She started stripping a month afterwards."

When you get back to the apartment, you're soaked with sun and music. You kick back on the couch and call home. Your father tells you your mother's staying at Aunt Viola's again. He doesn't say why until you ask how many bruises. Then he starts to cry.

On Sunday morning you sit up to find Maxim on the floor in your sleeping bag, wide-awake, quietly flipping through one of your magazines.

"Sleeping beauty awakens." He rises to give you a sleepy hug. You turn on the radio so you can talk. When you open your door, you hear sobbing from Sandra's room. You knock on her door, open it to find her crumpled on the bed in a t-shirt, tears blearing her face. On her arms and legs you see the raised welts, and long, bleeding scratches.

"I told you about making all that noise!"

"What noise? We were up all night talking, then Maxim fell asleep on the floor." You sit down on the bed next to her.

She grabs a tissue from a box on her nightstand, blows her nose, sighs. "When I was a kid my mother used to spend entire days in her bedroom with her boyfriends. I remember sometimes I'd be knocking on her door 'cause I was hungry and there'd be nothing to eat. But she wouldn't come out. I'd turn up the T.V. so I didn't have to hear anything."

You're stroking her shoulders while Sandra tells you about the laughing woman behind the bedroom door. She explains how it became normal and she got used to making sandwiches, how she'll never eat another sandwich in her life. The television got turned up so loud the neighbours downstairs complained. It was worth it. Anything so that she wouldn't have to hear that woman laughing and boyfriends coming and going, the noises of all the people in her mother's bedroom. She rolls into a ball.

You're sitting cross-legged on the bed when Maxim steps to the doorway with questioning eyes, then nods and leaves. Sandra sees this, gives you a quizzical look. "This is stupid," she says soberly, swatting tears. She picks up her furry heart-shaped phone book.

"I should call my dealer—Christ I need some weed."

The warm space cake sits half-eaten on the coffee table. Everybody's had a big slice with a glass of wine, so you'll be buzzing already when the cake starts working magic. The CD player changes from electronica to soul and you and Max start grooving on the couch. Moira laughs and pulls you onto your feet to dance with her. Sandra joins you while Max nods appreciatively at the three women dancing around him. The girls are laughing and you feel the space cake kick in and you're moving in slow motion. Maxim grins at you and you're elated. You remember Lily surrounded by the boys at the party. Max took a look at her and said, "Yeah she's cute. So?" He squeezed you like a plush toy. You are his "it girl". You twirl through the room, your skirt flirting around your thighs. You start to feel a little too disoriented for your own comfort and sit down on the couch opposite Max. The entire room is slowly revolving. Sandra does a tease dance for Max, her scarf already wrapped around his neck while she shakes her boobs in his face. They're both laughing and you feel claustrophobic, you need air. What are they doing? You see him get up and start dancing with her and you need to leave because you're not sure who exactly is being weird. You bound to your room and stand near the open window. Luckily there's no extra trash stinking up the fire escape or you wouldn't be able to lean out and draw in the cold night air. There's a forlorn cat sitting on the wrought iron steps that looks at you and meows, returns to licking its fur in thick chunks. Sandra can't help herself, you realize; seduction is her biggest fix. The chilled air fills your body and you can't help wondering how many times it has been yours.

You pull out your drawer, sweep all the lingerie to one side, grab all of the paddles, whips, chains, handcuffs. You stuff them into a plastic bag and you're ready to toss it out the window when you realize that the accessories themselves mean nothing: it's all about how they're used, who uses them.

You pick out the leather handcuffs, your favourite paddle and out goes the rest.

You're looking directly at the wall and picture a scene of the living room on the red and brown bricks, grab your sketchbook and scribble. Maxim strolls in and finds you on the bed.

Les Desmoiselles de l'Esplanade: Madam, Superdyke, and Chinoiserie

"You okay?" he asks. You nod. He looks at your drawing curiously.

"Hey is that me? It's pretty good..." He flips through a few pages, his half-cocked smile going off in laughter every now and then. Then he looks at you like you're wearing your hair differently and he can see a part of your face he's never noticed before. You haven't touched him yet. He hasn't asked, or even tried. As you show him the sketchbook, you feel him beside you, both of you quiet, just breathing.

Adam Bobbette

How to make some simple things impossibly thick

Ed. note

A version of this piece appeared on the website www.instructables.com, a site where users post step-by-step instructions for creating useful objects, or improving existing ones.

Hello everyone,

This is my first set of instructions. I hope they will be helpful and clear enough to understand. This is a machine I made that makes things impossibly thick (fig 1). The steps that follow are not perfect, there are variables. These variables should become obvious as you read the steps. There are a minimum of 10 steps, with a few subsidiary steps, to follow.

fig 1

fig 2

Step 1

February (or so), 1979: Conception
November 28, 1980. I was born in
Barrie, Ontario, Canada at the Royal
Victoria Hospital, a ten-story hospital
filled with many bodies and machines
and countless types of fluids. I am told
that the number of sperm present in
a man can vary greatly depending on
numerous factors (such as general
health, time of the month, or the presence of toxins). The body produces
new sperm all the time to replace
those that are expelled during ejacula-
tion, but they also have a very short life
span. There is one egg, though countless, unimaginable numbers of sperm,
and each one carries slightly different
DNA. The chance that any one sperm
will fertilize an egg is extremely low.
Conception is miraculous (fig 2).

Step 2

Montréal
My work room at home, in Montréal,
a city of 1.6 million people (as of 2006,
but this is just a statistic and we know
that statistics are only skeletons of
reality). Here is where I sometimes
make things. I move around and touch

and smell things. Glue them together, rummage, sometimes drill things and my phone is here, too. Yesterday, as I was working on this machine, my friend called. We talked for a while about interesting things. 25 minutes passed and I was 25 minutes longer in finishing the thickening machine (fig 3).

fig 3

Step 3

Glass and arguments
This glass, like most glass, is from the depths of the earth. It was once a vessel for pickles in a deli. My friend convinced the deli to give it to her and she used it in a theatre show. People who saw the show liked it. I think that she put a model of Percy Shelley's head in it, but I can't exactly remember.* She lent it to me. We used to hang out a lot, so she trusts me.

The pickle company bought it from Neston Glass. Sand fields in the southwest (USA) are filled with white sand blown in by winds coursing the planet. It is a really low area so the wind drops it there. This sand could be a composite of so many places: rock faces in Nepal, low-lying granite deposits in Vermont. I may have bits of Nepal in my living room; blind,

*Ed. note
It was her heart, actually. Which, due to long illness, had become calcified by the time he died. Percy Shelley literally had a heart of stone.

fig 4

dumb bits of Nepal. Sometimes things seem dumb to us because they won't betray their beginnings in a language we understand.

Neston Glass is in Nebraska. A woman named Yvonne Helder worked there for 12 years. Sometimes she monitored the bottles. She may have seen this pickle jar being made. Since it's well known that repetitive tasks have the power to induce daydreams, this jar may have been the last thing she noticed before she stopped paying attention to the jars and started daydreaming about her daughter. She may also have not even noticed this jar because she was already thinking about her daughter. Yvonne's parents were both born in Ohio (fig 4).

3b: The piece of glass on top of the jar was found in the street on my way home late one night after an argument. Our world is saturated in glass. I wish I knew how to make it. If anyone knows, I would love to hear it.

Step 4

Plexiglas

Plexiglas is strange. Its production process requires petroleum. Petroleum is thousands of years old and its creation requires the pushing and shoving of tectonic plates and fossil deposits. It also needs large industrial rollers to flatten molten chemical compounds, and a German immigrant named Ohm persuaded by the American dream (fig 5).

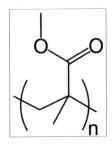

fig 5

Step 5

Hydro-Québec, Jacques Poincare, and the Chicago World's Fair
5a: Hydro-Québec flooded miles and miles of boreal forest in the 1980s. It is one of the biggest hydroelectric projects in the world. It's up there with the Three Gorges dam project in China.
5b: Jacques Poincare had little education, but loved life on the South Shore of Montréal (which itself was formed by glaciers travelling southward) and he drove the delivery truck that distributed electrical outlet casings to hardware stores. Jean Galliard talked often and bought the wrong cover while gossiping about his wife. They decided not to return it though.
5c: When electricity was demonstrated at the Chicago World's Fair, people thought they were witnessing a miracle (fig 6).

fig 6

Step 6

Cardboard

Cardboard. Just a little bit of it. For the existence of cardboard, you first of all need the existence of things that need to be contained. To account for the effluence of things, please see the industrial revolution and the emergence of commodity capitalism (fig 7).

fig 7

Step 7

Barrie North Collegiate

In the hallway at Barrie North Collegiate, my English teacher, Ms. Nyman, told me, "I worry about your lack of discipline."

Step 8

Uyen

Uyen, found herself living with her aunt and uncle in Shanwei and working at a knick-knack factory. Finkledy Tool and Die (Scarborough, Ontario) makes molds for some knick-knacks, including little couches. They ship them to China, including Shanwei. Uyen would watch as excess plastic was trimmed off knick-knacks (fig 8).

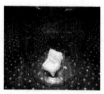

fig 8

Step 9

Things
Things. You need everything to make
a thing (fig 9).

Step 10

Thickness
Once it becomes clear that all things
inhere in one thing, we find ourselves
in an incredible thickness (fig 10).

fig 9

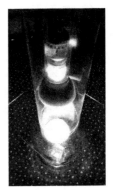

fig 10

Photo credits
Figure 7, courtesy of Carrie Barbash.
Figure 6, courtesy of Ryan Wakely.
All other images in this piece are courtesy of the author.

91

How to make some simple things impossibly thick

Ed's note

This is a little sum-uppy, if you know what I mean. The piece arrives there anyway, more or less, so I don't think you need to say it so categorically. Also, I hate 'we'. If you want to talk explicitly about the thickness, can you move from this to something about how the thickness doesn't stop here but keeps moving through all things, like specific things as well as abstract things? So maybe you can go from abstraction to specificity here as well. Maybe you need to talk about the machine a bit more.

Author's note

But I love 'we'. . .

Maybe what's not clear though is that you don't need a machine to make things thick because everything is already thick, illogically thick. The machine is just an arbitrary stacking of things; you can take any thing and start to retrace the infinity of chance causes that made it. And when I do I quickly come to this point where I say, I can't even fathom all the causes of the simplest little thing. It's almost as if there is an infinity contained in every little thing. And it doesn't stop. A thing keeps on moving, affecting things, causing other things to happen, other objects to emerge, and comments and perspectives ... Yeah, and then it's like some kind of implosion or something. I just have to say, ok so this is out of my ability to grasp and it's got to stop so I will just go back to a hammer being a hammer that hammers things, and a button being a button that holds my shirt together, not some unfathomable thickness held by a thread to my chest.

Editor's and Author's Note

On the following pages are the comments posted to this piece. We would like to thank those who posted their comments for not-so-knowingly adding to the thickness of this machine.

Comments

Larrylemon says: Psychological help is available. See www. psychologicalselfhelp.org. Although it is funny.

Boatgoball says: So, you have managed to shine a light on a plastic chair in a pickle jar, well done.

John Smith says: Oh god, is this that "art" crap? Come on, get a life. I've been too busy with my life to understand pointless stuff, sorry.

Binary Ronin says: but not too busy to post a pointless comment, eh?

John Smith says: I don't think my comment was pointless. I'm just saying that this website is for instructions, not THIS stuff. I wanted to see something cool, but what I got was a letdown.

Binary Ronin says: Please don't get me wrong, I too was let down by this "instructable". I was referring more to your statement regarding "that 'art' crap". As I am an artist (electronic media) myself, I really don't understand the ignorance inherent in a statement such as "that 'art' crap". Besides, you can't ignore the fact that several other 'ibles' are really pointless themselves. I'm thinking of all the "how to download free music" or the dozens of copycats who simply replicate someone else's work without demonstrating an improvement. I also think that if you find something mildly offensive like this, then why would you waste your time posting a non-constructive, critical comment? especially when your life is so "busy".

John Smith says: I don't know. Let's let this drop.

evilgamer63 says: wow that's something, um if i were you i would put the bong down.

John Smith says: Hahahaha, I agree.

mikeasauraus says:
1 - This isn't an instructable.
2 - Your machine looks broken, or incomplete.
3 - No one cares that you were born in the armpit of Canada.
4 - This isn't a forum for introspective storytelling.

rcjedi says: hee hee, you tell 'em!

shooby says: Yeah, worst Inst. I've ever seen. Doesn't say what you're making. All it is is a little couch in a jar. Please explain what the hell this is!

Lftndbt says: LOL... I REALLY think you have missed the point of this... along with most others...

saites2001: Just because it's "interesting" or "deep" does not mean it belongs here.

trebory6 says: I dont get it. What is this instructing me to do?I didnt learn how to make things thick at all. I know this is your first instructable, but I really don't know what its "Instructing" us to do. =\

GorillazMiko says: is this a story or something? Because i wanted to make a penny really thick.

Erik Lindemann says: Is this a riddle of sorts? Does this life story end up leading into this thickening machine or what? I'm sorry, but I just don't understand this. Maybe I'm thick.

Sue Carter Flinn

Open House

"Do you like classic rock?"

"No. Not really."

"Sorry. It's all we have."

The man, who refers to himself only as "Your Technician", but looks more like a roadhouse waiter, places the headphones over my ears, their soft weight pressing against the sides of my skull. Fleetwood Mac's *Go Your Own Way* cuts in and out, angry static filling space.

Up close, the MRI machine is not that impressive. A child's bed suspended through the eye of a needle. What does scare me is the absence. No stuff. There isn't a chair, a desk or even an encouraging poster on the wall.

I twist a phantom ring. I had to sign a waiver and take off all my metal, my bra, even my nose stud, which I never do because I'm scared of infections and the hole closing up. Not sure what happens if I leave the stud in; no one tells you that. Maybe I'd end up hanging nose-first from the ceiling or microwaved from the inside out. Or maybe it just fucks up the expensive machinery.

Technician lifts my knees onto a foam triangle and fixes the pillow under my head. A heavy plastic-armoured plate is placed on my tummy. He is gentle and efficient, I'll give him that.

Aerosmith. Lame.

"I'm going into the booth now. Give me a signal if you need anything."

For this he gets a thumbs up and an eye roll.

From behind the safety of his glass booth, Technician's voice filters through the headphones, momentarily blocking out the histrionic singing. The bed jerks slightly, then slides through the middle of the hole, like some kind of rude hand gesture. Inside, the tube is dark except for strips of bright green lights, glowing festively like a miniature discotheque.

My sister Anna has dyed black hair and bad skin. It gives her the appearance of an old fashioned rag doll, neglected and stained. Every Saturday she goes to the tanning salon in the strip mall near our apartment on St. Clair, but I can never tell the difference. Anna says that the tanning bed relaxes her, but maybe that's because she smokes pot with the receptionist beforehand in the alley. Small spaces and weed don't make me feel cozy, just confined.

There is something growing on my ovary that shouldn't be. My doctor says that the MRI is just a precaution because I am young and most likely it's nothing but a blur. But we need to be sure, especially because of my family's history. She refuses to say anything else until the tests are done, and advises me to stay away from the Internet. It's full of hypochondriacs and nut jobs, the doctor says, handing me a crude drawing she made of my misshapen ovaries on the back of a smoking cessation brochure. My left ovary looks like it's wearing a giant, floppy sun hat.

"The tests are no big deal. You'll be okay," Anna said dismissively over Pop-Tarts this morning, obsessively scraping the jam off the biscuits with a fork. Anna only eats food out of boxes and plastic wrapping. Anything she puts in her mouth, she likes to know where it came from.

"I should know; I'm the one with the hospital bills, remember? Hey, maybe it has teeth and hair. Like that Margaret Atwood story. You can name him Harry or Tommy the Tumour. Meet me after?"

"Ha, ha, ha. No way. I'll name it after her auntie, Anna the Annoying. And yes."

Without warning from Technician, an alarm blasts through the room, filling the tube with excruciating sound. I shove my fingers between the headphones and my ears to block the nuclear whistle.

Then momentary quiet. An even louder bell, like a school fire drill, takes its place. Silence again. Aerosmith. Technician says something about holding my breath and the alarm starts again. We begin a strange tango: Breathe in. Hold it. Alarm. Silence. Dream On. Sing it with me, turn me into a giant magnet today. Maybe tomorrow the good Lord will take you away.

After fifteen minutes, Technician emerges. He presses a button and the bed slides back out. He removes the plate from my chest and helps me up from the bed.

"That's it. You'll hear back from your doctor in the next couple of weeks with the results."

Not sure what happens next, so I hold out my hand. He awkwardly accepts, like the end of a platonic date. We have no chemistry, Technician and me. For the first time, I notice his hairy sausage fingers and the oversized gold ring with the X sliced down the middle.

I quickly slip my bra back on, and push the stud back in my nose. Outside in the lobby, a fatigued young Spanish woman explains to a nurse that she doesn't need any help.

"Oh, we know what happens now. She's an old pro, aren't you, honey?"

The woman nods her head at a curly-haired toddler sitting on the floor, gnawing on the tail of a plastic cow. I know this look. Years of Mom annoyed, tired of the routine, briskly explaining to well-meaning doctors, nurses and specialists that Anna would be "just fine" coping with another set of tests or IV poke.

The MRI clinic is housed in the middle of the ultrasound department—an unfortunate planning error, really—so I instinctively assume the arched-back stance of a pregnant woman under my coat. Our family is allergic to sympathetic looks.

Since she was 18, Anna has refused to go anywhere near a hospital. I pull out the piece of paper she shoved in my purse this morning. "Take the College streetcar to Ossington. 20-A Delaware. XOXOX!!!"

Relieved that I don't have to take the subway, I wait for a streetcar, flipping the token around inside my mitten. Lately the combined underground smell of wet wool and newsprint from the free papers tossed onto the subway floor makes me feel panicky.

I take a seat near the window. I pop two pills that I stole from Anna's stash, and immediately feel calmer, memories of the hospital evaporating into the clunky sounds of the streetcar track. At College and Spadina, the car fills with elderly Asian shoppers loaded with mesh bags overflowing with rooty vegetables, goth kids with their chipped black nail polish and attitudes, and oblivious hipsters staring glassy-eyed into their cell phones as busy thumbs do all the work. I take two more pills, washing them down with a bottle of water from my purse.

When I reach Delaware, I look for the sign: Open House. Today.

Anna is already waiting out front. She pulls me in for a hug, while jumping up and down. The only thing that my sister loves more than her weekly tan-and-bake are open houses. After she turned eighteen, and got her first adult bill of clean health, she started dating Dave, a real estate agent who was twice her age. Dave would take Anna to bars where, as she explained to me afterwards, she'd sit on high stools, sipping sweet martinis adorned with lichee nuts and gold cinnamon flakes. Then Dave would drive her to his empty houses and they would screw on impressively renovated granite countertops and updated, modern bathroom vanities. Once, she confessed that he liked to kiss the scar on her chest where the catheter used to live. The affair ended abruptly—something to do with his wife and a surly apple-shaped bruise that appeared on Anna's forearm—but she was left with an insatiable lust for open houses and a sharp eye for shoddy repairs.

"So here's the scoop: A beautiful Victorian home in a mature neighbourhood. Extremely well kept and maintained. New furnace. Quiet, private. Steps away from TTC and shopping. One owner, new roof, prime location!"

Anna pirouettes and play-punches me in the side of the head. I grab her hand and follow a young family up to the house. She whispers something about Portuguese neighbours and their insistence on picking ugly front doors, and it's my turn to punch her in the head.

"Welcome, ladies."

A tall, heavyset woman in a pressed red suit is already annoyed by our presence. Our matching black curls and second-hand peacoats do not suggest owner potential.

"I'm Lydia Thomas. If you need anything, let me know. Feel free to take a look around. There's some literature by the door."

Ol' Lydia moves towards the family, intimately placing one manicured hand on the man's back and another one on their drooling baby's blond head. We remove our boots and follow the gleaming plastic runners into the living room, a confection of lavender and yellow doilies. All of the photos have been removed, leaving ghostly etchings on the walls; the only signs of human existence are tiny pencil marks on a doorframe noting a child's growth.

Anna tsks. "Check out the crap wallpaper in the living room. Look how it's peeling near the ceiling. If they had steamed it off and repainted, it would add at least a few thou to the asking price."

The odour of baked bread coming from the kitchen—Anna says they use it to cover the smell of old people decaying—makes my stomach rise and fall.

"Anna, I think I might be sick."

"What? You can't barf in a $649,000 living room."

"$649? That's ridiculous. Who can afford to live in this city? Seriously. I'm going outside to get some air."

She shrugs and lets me go to examine the original stone fireplace. Instead of going outside, I run up a flight of stairs and quietly slip into a washroom and lock the door. The floor—miniature checked black and white porcelain tiles, an upgrade obviously—feels cool against my cheek. I take the last two pills out of my purse and swallow without water. I want to be home, sitting at our rusting Formica table, listening to the hum of the refrigerator that never completely defrosts. In the summer we climb out the kitchen window onto the fire escape to drink beer, Anna reading out MLS ads from her laptop while I nod at all the right words.

Whenever we fight, she threatens to leave. Buy a faux-hemian loft on Queen West with vessel sinks, security cameras and an indoor dog park. But I know she won't go. After Dave, after the month when she refused to talk to anyone, after the web of scars on the inside of her thighs healed, she made me promise I'd never leave. We have a deal.

I imagine Tommy the Tumour pushing his way out of my chest to freedom. He has dark curly hair, twisted and wrapped around his body, forming an X. I don't make it in time, the watery contents of my empty stomach release onto the clean floor.

"Excuse me, miss. Are you all right in there? Are you able to open the door?"

I can't answer. My tongue is swollen and dry. I heave again but nothing comes out. Lydia's polite taps on the door speed up to a frantic banging. I hear Anna's voice coming up the stairs, discussing the merits of hardwood versus carpet with the young husband.

"Sis? Checking out the bathroom? New floors apparently… how are they?"

"I think your sister is sick. Can you help her?"

Anna whispers something to Lydia, who ushers the family down the stairs towards the new deck and outdoor calming fountain.

"It's just me, okay. Open the door?"

Shivering, I crawl towards the door and flick the latch. Anna falls to the floor beside me.

"Wow." Anna laughs softly, pressing her hand against her nose. "You did a number in here. Way to knock the price down. Better than that *Brady Bunch* scam, when the kids haunted the house so no one would buy it. Bet Marcia never thought of puking all over it. Remember how much we loved that show?"

My words slur. "You're not funny. I'm sick and all you can do is make dumb house jokes. For once, just once in your life, can you help me?"

"Taking care of others isn't exactly one of my finer qualities, you know that. It comes with the territory. I was born with this illness."

We listen as the new furnace kicks in and the radiator starts clanging like a heartbeat. I pass out as Anna pulls me to her lap, wrapping her coat gently around my back.

Teri Vlassopoulos

How Things Grow

In a city, particularly around the edge of a city, there is a network of structures dedicated to noise abatement. It's always baffling to realize that there are whole industries built around things we can barely imagine having enough material to fill their own trade journals—asphalt, joints used in bridges that allow the girders to swell and buckle with the changes in the weather—but they do. Monthly.

For a city's population, noise abatement is important, the kind of thing that has a direct impact on efficiency and productivity, the kind of thing that, unlike other variables, can be measured and controlled. When houses started getting built near highways, and when highways became burdened by all those cars, something had to be done about the noise. So they built walls.

You see the walls along highways, long expanses of concrete stretching out towards the horizon, blocking the surrounding landscape. Or, maybe you don't see them at all —they just blend into your general idea of a highway. These walls are usually only noticed in the context of something unusual, like that snowy December morning I drove from Toronto back to Montréal and watched in wonder as the car a few hundred metres ahead of me bounced slowly along the highway. I realized that it had slipped on a patch of ice, and as the car repeatedly bashed itself into the concrete wall I wondered why on earth someone would erect such a hard, unfriendly structure along an icy highway.

The answer: noise abatement.

But even before that morning, I had thought about these walls. Andrew pointed them out. For a while he had this idea to photograph them, different ones in different cities. Point out their differences. Some cities have sober, grey walls. Others are more whimsical, like the ones along the 20E out of Montréal with little geometric detailing along the edges. Do sound barrier walls say something about the city? I've taken to paying attention to the parts of a city that snap everything together. Like, sewer lines. Street lights.

When you're in a forest or a big field or walking along a river you are acutely aware of growth. Crumbling dirt, buzzy insects, the rustle of dead leaves falling away from their branches. But in a city, you forget about this process. Things just pop up, like that new coffee shop on the corner, which was a *pho* restaurant two months ago, and an Irish pub six months before that. An entire subdivision, all houses sold, appears in the empty lot you drove by a month ago on your way to visit your parents. Occasionally a city's growth is hard to ignore. Maybe the street you walk along to get to work every morning has been under construction for the past few months or your water has been temporarily shut off so that work can be done on the pipes outside. It's still hard to conceptualize this kind of nuisance as growth. It's not as pretty, I guess. But it's hard to look at those old, grainy photos of your city from barely thirty years ago and not be shocked by how the empty spaces have filled up so tightly and quickly.

I have a map of Toronto from the seventies that I keep in my car. Downtown, there is a blank space, and a caption that just says "planned domed stadium".

To grow a stop sign you need the rest of the neighbourhood to agree they want one. Maybe you get a petition going to make sure. You have to make a few calls to the councillor in your ward, invite him to a neighbourhood meeting. You need to find out when the city council holds its meetings. It helps if you find an engineer in your neighbourhood, or someone who knows an engineer who specializes in urban planning, and have her draw up some plans, make a few calculations, drum up some scientific evidence to prove that the stop sign is necessary at that particular intersection. At a council meeting you have to make a presentation. If you're lucky, if the votes are in your favour, eventually, months later, you will have that stop sign.

My parents' neighbourhood got one like that. It happened a few years ago, after I moved out. I still forget it's there, accustomed to years of cruising down the street and pulling into the driveway in one fluid motion. Whenever I visit my parents, I skid to a stop too late, cringing as I imagine the dead children crushed under the car wheels.

Maybe it's obvious to most people that a city is nested on a system of roots, held together by a skeleton that breaks and expands and fuses back together, but this is something I've only begun to notice, get interested in. Not necessarily because of the new growth, the depressing mindless expansion of the suburbs, but because of the remains of the older stuff, the things that were planted first.

Andrew takes photos of the abandoned parts of various Rust Belt cities, of declining industrial towns. You wouldn't believe the sheer size of these abandoned factories, how packed they are with broken tile and bricks, clumps of asbestos, rusted gears. These rotting buildings are easily beautiful in their decay, the way a rotting tree is starkly beautiful in a forest. But there are also the factories and office buildings that remain unchanged from the last day they were in operation. These are the ones that were shut down in, say, 1994 or 2001, the fall of 2005. It's as if the employees were told to leave as fast as they could and no one bothered to shut their ledger books, cap their pens or empty their lockers. The cubicle walls were never disassembled, the schedules and reminders never wiped off the dry erase boards.

Some rooms still contain boxes and boxes of documents. Once Andrew brought me home a stack of issued permits for the Buffalo Memorial auditorium. The stadium opened in 1940 and closed in the mid-nineties, and is still sitting there waiting for its eventual demolition. In the meantime, if you're persistent you might be able to get in and stand at centre ice. My favourite permit is granted by the City of

Buffalo to the Mystic Order of Veiled Prophets of the Enchanted Realm for their use of the auditorium. Dated April 29, 1957.

But I mean, this stuff, it just languishes there. You enter these darkened buildings, flip a light switch and see it all before you. The power is often kept on, as if someone in their rush to leave forgot to tell the hydro company what had happened.

I haven't been to many of these places, sometimes preferring to look at the pictures, hear about them, read about them. I'm still sometimes a little afraid of their eerie silence. Their sadness. When confronted with something this huge and forgotten it makes you realize that the amount of space you take up, the fact that you take up space at all, is not directly proportionate to your value. Your tangible self, when deemed irrelevant, is not destroyed, but simply ignored. I know they're just buildings. But.

Some buildings are easier to get into than others, like the Brickworks in Toronto, a sprawling former brick factory off the Don Valley Expressway. You squeeze in between some loose boards and hope that you don't get pierced by rusty nails, and on a summer day, the insides are cool and quiet, the sunlight filtering in from the broken windows and worn roof.

Dow Brewery is a big, abandoned brewery in Old Montréal. Like the Brickworks, it's a popular location if you're into exploring a certain kind of dusty, forgotten aesthetic. These are urban-exploring-for-beginners kinds of places. There are always rainbow-hued graffiti tags arcing across the walls, proof of the disconnect between what these buildings were once used for—molding bricks, fermenting beer—and what we use them for now—a background for art, or, less poetically and more realistically, the setting for aimless loitering. Parks with less people milling about.

When I visited Dow, it was a mid-summer Saturday night. We had out of town visitors and we wanted to show them the city, a different perspective of it. Armed with flashlights, our small group climbed up the dark stairs to the roof, ignoring the inside and its broken-down machinery. Someone had a bottle of wine tucked into their bag. It was misty out, but warm, and a late summer rainstorm had kept other people away, so it was just the five of us in the entire complex. There was a fireworks displaying going on, but by the time we got to the top of the building the last of the fireworks were shooting out from La Ronde, these showering red and yellow and green lights in the distance. We forgot to bring cups for the wine and took swigs from the bottle, passing it back and forth.

We split up, everyone poking around different areas of the roof. I looked over the edge of the building down to the street below and my stomach lurched a little, the way it used to when I would climb trees when I was younger, hugging a thick branch and visualizing the distance between my body and the ground. I edged back and shuffled along the broken tiles and clumps of mud to join the rest of the group. Up there, we didn't talk much, and when we did, our voices were low. The evening passed slowly and we kept catching each other curiously peering into the bloom of Montréal's darkened skyline the way someone might look into an empty mug to analyze tea leaves. The constellation of lights from downtown buildings, newly built condos and street lights formed a pattern. We hoped, if we stared at long enough would tell us something, if not about the future, then maybe the past.

Molly Lynch

In Public

I had to break the ice on the well that morning when it was still dark. Dropping the pail alone wouldn't do it so I had to go get a stone from by the woodshed, even though Dad told me about a thousand times not to use stones. My breath glowed white in the dark morning and the cold air seared my face. The snow walls of the path were as high as my shoulders. "It's too effing frozen Mom!" I yelled at the house as I trundled down to the woodshed. Whether or not they heard me didn't matter and I knew it. I was going to have to get the water myself if I wanted to wash my hair. And I didn't just want to. I *needed* to. And then I needed to get it totally dry so I could brush and spray my bangs up and back. Not quite like what a curling iron would do but as close as I could get without having a curling iron—or electricity.

I thought it was really un-funny that Mel K. now had a Braun cordless, as well as a plug-in, not to mention an electrical outlet in her warm bedroom. Her bedroom, with its touch lamp and peach carpets that swallowed your bare feet, just down the hall from a living room with remote control television and only a few paces away from the fully equipped kitchen with running water, self-igniting stove and vertical refrigerator. She thought it was funny that I thought it was so un-funny. Whatever. At least she brought her Braun to school and I could redo my bangs at lunchtime basically every day.

I found a stone the size of a small skull and cradled it against my chest as I tromped back up to the well, trying not to trip over my nightgown with my felt-pack boots. At the well I paused for a moment before pushing the stone over the edge. I let it fall and listened to it burst satisfyingly through that top layer before sinking down to the dark icy bottom. I hauled up three pails and then managed to carry the basin all the way back in the dark without getting soaked. Obviously I knew every step of that path by heart.

Luckily, Mom had been up since five or something and the fire was already raging. As I kicked the creaking door shut behind me I muttered to her that the well was totally frozen even with the lid on it and that the last person to bed at night should really go and drop the pail in it every night now that it was so retardedly cold if they really didn't want people to throw rocks in the well.

Her large square glasses gleamed in the lamplight and she looked at me from between the curtains of her long hair that she kept flat and parted directly down the middle as if she lived to embarrass me. "Please speak a bit nicer this morning, Odette." I rolled my eyes as deep and slow as I could. I felt her studying my face. She sighed and wiped the dough off her hands and came over to help me empty the basin into the pot and we hoisted it up onto the stove together.

"So," she said to me. "Are you going to be just as friendly to all the kids at school today as you are to me?"

"We're not kids actually."

"Oh right..." she said slowly. "I almost forgot. Teenagers... of course. That explains everything..."

I rolled my eyes again and turned away. I already knew everything she was thinking. About "tone of voice," about being "respectful," et cetera. I went to let out Loki and Kisha who were jumping all over each other at the back door. I decided to give my mom silent treatment while I ate my Cheerios with hot milk and honey and waited for my water to heat up.

Eating Cheerios made me feel calm. It wasn't quite Captain Crunch, but it also wasn't no-name puffed wheat that came in a gigantic sack that never ended. And it wasn't a bunch of oats and grains stewed in a big pot, that your mom or dad told you would make your cheeks rosy; and then you ended up in a discussion about why plain, beige cheeks were better than big fat red ones; then both of your parents laughed and laughed about the idea of "plain, beige cheeks"; and they tried to make you laugh too and you almost did. You had to try your hardest not to crack a smile.

Dad came downstairs buttoning up his shirt and tucking it into his work pants. He was cheery and started joking right away about how I better get my hair washed quick so that my bangs wouldn't freeze and crack off on my way to the bus stop. Everything seemed to be all about my hair those days. My parents teased me about it constantly and tried to argue that some day I would grow out of my hair-spray habit. They told me that some day I'd look back on it and laugh.

"There's just no way," I insisted. "There's just no way." And I knew I was right. I was so totally serious when I said that if I were stranded all alone on a desert island, even with nobody else there to see me, the one thing I would want most would be a brush and a bottle of Final Net and a Braun curling iron. They told their friends about that one. I swear to god everything those days was about my hair.

Through the big windows that faced the silent frozen forest I could see the light starting to fill up the sky. I had to start washing and I had to do it fast because by the time I got everything ready Dad would be gone and there would be no way of getting a ride to the bus stop unless Mom drove me in the orange truck. I basically refused to be seen getting in or out of that truck. Sometimes I literally crouched on the floor when we drove through town.

And then it was done. My hair was washed, dried and styled. The day was blinding. Raven and Jupiter McArthur were already at the bus stop when I reached the top of the road. We all muttered hi to each other and then we stood scraping the toes of our boots into the packed snow. Now that Earth Voice School had been closed down and we all went to public school we didn't talk to each other anymore. Well, not at the bus stop or at school anyway. Our families still had plenty of political meetings and pot-lucks, and we kids would play cards or board games with each other. Only a week before, my family had gone to dinner at the McArthur house. The three of us had played with a ouija board on Raven's bedroom floor and we ended up rolling around terrified and in hysterics. So it wasn't like we didn't like each other. It was just that we totally understood that we had to have public school friends now. Raven had Colleen and Shantella. I had Mel K. and Mel M. Jupiter was a boy and in grade six so it didn't matter.

The staccato rattle of a woodpecker echoed from the woods. A truck with chains on the tires and a German Shepherd in the back roared up the road past us leaving a cloud of diesel fumes that I inhaled with pleasure. You could see chimney smoke rising up from behind the trees. I carved a deep crescent into the snow with the pointy toe of my black boot, pulled off my mitt and lightly touched the hard ridge of my upturned bangs. The bright yellow bus appeared, rumbling over the crest of the hill.

I quickly scanned the bus when I got on without catching anyone's eye. All the primary school kids were writhing around in snowsuits in the front seats. A couple of grade five girls stared at me from the middle. The high schoolers in the back were looking down, or out the window, aloof, paying no attention to grade seveners like me or Raven.

That morning we had art first block. Since I got to public school people started saying I was really good at art. They would stand over my shoulder and say "Aww... Holy... How do you know how to do that?" I didn't mind. At Earth Voice nobody would do that seeing as basically everyone was good at art there. And that was probably because "creative exploration of our world through colour, music and the physical experience" was what Earth Voice was supposed to be all about—as well as "honesty, generosity and respect for others". We did our math with stuff like paint and crayons, wood, yarn and chestnuts. When we learned about gradients we went outside and climbed hills. When we learned about circumferences and diameters we found trees and stumps. That was what my mom, who had been the math teacher there, called the "visual and physical approach."

That was before it all changed, when basically a lot of new people came to put their kids in Earth Voice because they had heard about the school. They were all really "gung-ho" as Mom said. Like the couple named Charmene and Carl who came from California where they had worked at a Waldorf school and wanted to work at Earth Voice even though they didn't have any kids. My parents went to meetings all the time then. I started hearing so much about "alternative teaching techniques" and Waldorf. A lot of people wanted Earth Voice to be more Waldorf. I didn't really get it. I just heard that they didn't want us to wear shirts with words on them, which my mom said was "fascist." All the adults kept talking about how Earth Voice needed money and then some parents started to put their kids in public school. It was at the end of grade five that Earth Voice became "The Waldorf school." My parents were really upset about Charmene and Carl and other people who they said just wanted power. But then the McArthurs decided to put Raven and Jupiter in public school and my parents said they thought it was time for me to go too. I guess I was scared at first. I still wore my hair totally flat. I didn't even know about hairspray yet.

That morning after art block we had social studies. We were learning about GNP and under-developed, developing and developed countries. Then for "what's on the news" we got to watch a video of the Berlin Wall because it had just come down. I didn't quite get why the Berlin Wall had been there or why it was such a big deal that it was coming down. I was just glad that we got to watch a video.

Finally it was lunchtime. The Mels and I went to the gym bathroom that nobody used, to do our bangs with the Braun. I wet mine and then used the hand dryer to blow them dry. I had two rows of high-formed curls that I had lightly combed out to give a bit of a feathery look to and then sprayed. Mel K. just reinforced her already perfect blonde shiny rows. Those days Mel M. was into backcombing her bangs but I thought that looked bad on her because she had black hair and the dried hairspray would show up flaky and white in it. Mel K. and I didn't tell her but we both thought Mel M.'s style of doing her hair was bad.

"Let's totally *not* go outside," Mel K. said.

"Yeah." Mel M. and I totally agreed. I took tiny bites of my cheese and tomato sandwich and kept its brown bread hidden from the world in its tinfoil wrapper. I had fruit leather from the health-food store. Both Mels had real fruit roll-ups. We talked about whether or not we believed that Tanya had now had her period and took turns listening to *Straight Up* by Paula Abdul on Mel M.'s Walkman. I wished so bad that I could have just listened to it on a blasting stereo and danced and danced and danced with nobody watching. Mel K. updated me on what was happening on *Generations*. Adam was now having an affair with Laura-Lee. On Friday I would be able to watch the actual show when I went to stay the night at her house. I couldn't wait. We'd watch ITV sitcoms until *Generations* came on and then more sitcoms like *Who's the Boss* and *Family Ties*. After dinner her mom and step-dad would go out to the bar—to get loaded, as

Mel liked to say—and I could open and close the fridge door as I pleased just to stare into its lit-up inner world. Its Philadelphia cream-cheese, sweet pickles, Cool Whip, Molly McButter, whatever. We'd eat Old Dutch ripple chips with French Onion flavour dip and probably watch a video that her mom would rent for us. Maybe even *Look Who's Talking Too*.

As we were sitting on the steps by the library, Travis, Kevin, and Zack came up and started horsing around by the heaters near us. They each wore their baseball cap perched at the back of their head with their bangs sticking out the front. Zack had been in Earth Voice for grade five and six but he'd been asked to leave because of the three strikes you're out rule for using violence. He'd come to public a year before me. Even though this was already my second year in public he still seemed to think he was like a thousand times better than me and had called me a hippie once really loud in the gym and asked where my rubber boots were.

Travis came up to us and made a fist with his baby finger and thumb sticking out on either side. As he waggled it in front of us he asked us if we knew what it meant. Both Mels said, "Yeah, of course." I nodded and then looked down. Then I accidentally looked up and happened to catch Zack's eye.

"She doesn't know," he pointed at me.

I gave him the look with my eyebrows pinched together and my face in pain that was meant to say, "Oh my god you are so pathetic." But when I swallowed painfully I could feel all their eyes on me. Even the Mels'.

"What does it mean?" Travis grinned at me.

I could feel my heart pounding and I shrugged and gave him the "you're so pathetic" look and then flashed it at

Kevin too. Kevin, who was nice and hot, was also the only one not laughing and dangling his fist in my face.

"What does it mean?" Mel M. asked quietly. Mel K. started giggling. I rolled my eyes and looked away from all of them and said "Whatever!" and Travis was basically spazzing out by then with his stupid fist sign wagging everywhere.

"She totally doesn't know!" Zack wheezed and pointed.

"Yeah well who cares!" I stood up and stared at him. "Like who really cares? It's not like you know a lot! It's not like you're something totally cool and rad!" I grabbed my reusable lunch bag and turned away from all of them and huffed down the hall.

I went into the bathroom in the primary wing and stared at my face in the mirror. I touched my bangs. At least they were perfect. They looked so perfect to me that day. I went to the wall by the radiator and slid my back down and sat there with my knees pulled up to my chest. Then the door opened and a grade oneer or twoer came in. She had glasses and jagged bangs and the crotch of her fuzzy brown tights stretched below the hem-line of her dress. She stopped when she saw me and for a moment stood there staring and breathing heavily through her mouth.

"Hi," I said quietly.

She smiled a little and I saw that she was missing her front teeth. "Hi," she said and kept staring at me. "Are you a teenager?" she eventually asked.

"Yeah," I nodded. "Yeah... Thirteen."

"Oh..." she kept staring, breathing heavily through her open mouth. She cocked her head to the side then awkwardly reached up and touched her bangs. I smiled at her a little and then she smiled a little back. She began to walk slowly past me, staring at me the whole time until she closed the stall door behind her. I felt the warmth of the electric radiator. I touched my bangs. And then the warning bell rang.

Stephen Guy

To Some Lighthouse

Matthew Mugford walked to the lighthouse in Brigus with this woman, Melissa Warford, joking loudly about his inability to keep his ankles from rolling while scaling the broken-shale-covered side of the hill. She smiled absently but could not laugh, although the reason she had chosen Matthew over Darryl or Shane was his filthy sense of humour and pathetic grin. His sneakers were grey with age and both split identically at the top on back. He had borrowed his cousin's school bag and rolled up a blanket from the basement and stuffed it in, along with three bottles of beer and two condoms. Now he planted his feet deliberately on the narrow path worn by meandering goats and tried to conceal his fear of sliding with the shale down the hill and over the cliff and into Brigus harbour. Melissa allowed herself to bitterly hate her fiancé, Jeff Mugford, and danced lightly down the path behind Matthew.

Soon Brigus receded behind them, ninety barren minutes away. At the lighthouse Matthew unfurled the blanket over the brown grass and Melissa began to matter-of-factly remove her unstylish jeans. Matthew paused to watch her fold the jeans and place the neat square on top of a lichen-covered rock before struggling out of his stained sweatshirt. He had noticed the underpants Melissa was wearing on her clothesline last week. They were green and pink and looked expensive and strange, as if they had been ordered from a catalogue rather than grabbed from the sale bin at Wescal's in the strip mall in Bay Roberts. Melissa turned away from him and he noticed that they sagged in the rear, at least a size too big. She looked across the water and removed the underpants and enjoyed the way the wind made the small hairs stand on her thighs, then hooted loudly to hear the echo. Matthew laughed at the rend in the secret. He remembered Jeff complaining about how often Melissa embarrassed him by clowning publicly at high volume and considered yet again how thoughtless and criminally boring his brother was. Melissa wrinkled her forehead. Matthew guessed this was a signal and he reached for her hip.

While they were having sex on the blanket, Melissa stared up at the mass of grey clouds moving towards Brigus and imagined that her hatred was wind at a high altitude. Matthew had been preparing to enjoy this moment for years, or at least weeks, but now all he could think about was asking his neighbour for a ride to Bay Roberts tomorrow. He tried to concentrate on the warm and the wet but he could only feel the detailed and abstract shame of bumming a ride. Melissa grabbed two handfuls of flesh and murmured "yeah" a few times to spare his feelings but he barely noticed—he couldn't get the boiled cabbage leftovers smell of his neighbour's car out of his mind and everything was ruined. Matthew's behind shuddered and he gasped and it was over. He rolled onto his back and felt the damp of the grass press through the blanket. Melissa put her sneakers on and stood up and wandered over to the edge of the cliff. It occurred to him that naked people in sneakers look ridiculous. He put his own sneakers on and grabbed two bottles of beer from his cousin's schoolbag and grabbed the damp blanket and stood next to Melissa. She took a bottle and opened it and helped him drape the blanket around their shoulders to block the breeze. He opened his own bottle and they saluted one another with the bottles before drinking, their backyard barbecue rapport shakily restored.

"We look stupid," he said, staring at the toes of his sneakers, barely visible beyond his protruding stomach and the soggy flap of his cousin's blanket. He gestured towards her feet with his beer bottle.

She looked at his sneakers and at her own sneakers and took a pull from her bottle and said "Yes, Matt, we do." She winced and drank and watched the clouds hang grey and flat and still.

J.B. Staniforth

What's Left

The ride takes me almost an hour. When I arrive I see Hugh's bike locked to a street sign a half-block down from where we're supposed to meet, so I lock mine to his and walk on. The mid-afternoon sun is hot; the skin on my face feels swollen and sweaty and my eyes are rimmed with dust from the road. I try to wipe it away and succeed only in rubbing it in. My lips are dry and chapped and I wish I'd brought a bottle of water.

There's no one on the street and as far as I can tell there's no one at home in any of the houses for a few blocks. The lawns are mowed, but the driveways are empty. Somewhere in the trees or bushes a pair of cicadas are trading two pitches of dentist-drill buzzing on and off. In the silence that's left, I can hear the distant hum of traffic on the main road a few streets away and nothing beyond it.

Hugh told me that they built the suburbs out this far in the sixties, then just stopped and left them here. The city continued building east and west; some zoning regulation kept it from moving south. A few blocks beyond this point there are only scattered squares of industrial park, then undeveloped land, highway, and the beginning of the country. Unlike the newer neighbourhoods in the east and west, however, the houses here look like *buildings*—they're made with brick, stone, wood, and shingles, squat and long and built to last. Some have been kept in the condition in which they must have begun, but most show varying degrees of wear. There are missing bricks and patches of peeling paint, and a few have front porches that are clearly collapsing, planks of old wood bloated with rot. Only one house has boarded windows rimmed with black scorches and overgrown bushes all around it. That's where Hugh is waiting.

I walk up the driveway to find him lurking around the corner in the long and weedy grass of the backyard. His cargo shorts are too big, and even with his mint-green golf shirt tucked in, he seems like a sliver of guy inside them. Only his curly amber hair, unkempt and dense and drifting to near-afro range, offers some size in his favour. Beneath the hair, his little green eyes seem like jittery buttons not sewn on tight enough. He's got a knapsack and a tote bag.

"Man, what took you so long?" he says excitedly. "There's people around!"

"No there aren't," I say.

"There was a guy driving up and down the road earlier. He was watching me when I rode past."

"How many times did he go by?"

Hugh thinks a second. "Only twice, I guess. But you should have seen the look he gave me. He could tell I was up to something."

Hugh's four years older than me, a year out of high school, and better than me at physics. He's better than most people at physics, but beyond that he isn't good at many things. With advice from his father, he's putting university off at least a year so he can experience a bit of the world and save some money. So far, most of the money he's made he's spent on weed, computer equipment, and bike parts, and he's spent the majority of his time alone on his bike, exploring the outer rim of the city where the railroad tracks are. Hugh knows as much about trains as he does about physics. And fireworks.

At first, I didn't want to be friends with Hugh on account of what a huge fucking nerd he was. I used to see him on the bus with his socks pulled up most of the way to his shorts and this weird brace that held the straps of his knapsack together. When everybody would get off at school, he'd charge off like the storm-trooper of the geeks, ten times as fast as everyone else with a posture of the most serious intent you'd ever seen. Years ahead of all of us, he was none-theless well-known in our grade as King Nerd.

I was flunking physics and my dad sent me over to his friend Ron's so Ron's kid could tutor me, but I had no idea it was going to be Hugh. He opened the door wearing brown cords and a black and white plaid shirt buttoned up to the collar and I think I actually groaned out loud. If I did, I'm sorry—he's an okay guy, even if he is a dork, and I guess

I'm lucky to have him, since he's introduced me to some neat shit.

The thing about physics is that some people understand it instinctively and can't explain it, but there are other people who can explain it to you from an outside perspective. Even though physics was never natural to me, Hugh explained each part so I *got* it rather than just making me memorize the shit I needed for the exam. I was surprised by how much I *understood*, and how Hugh seemed to know how to get me from knowing nothing to knowing something. You can't help but respect someone who does that for you. Needless to say, Hugh did his job and I passed my class.

We started hanging out after my tutorials because of the firecrackers. With loving patience, Hugh spent hours dismantling dozens, hundreds, of individual fireworks so that he could consolidate their gunpowder into what he called "devices", large bombs made out of marker casings or film canisters. These he would use to blow stuff up—virtually anything that didn't serve him an immediate purpose—in his backyard. At first he sold me his "devices" cheap, but soon enough he taught me how to make them myself, with even greater care and zeal than that with which he taught me physics. It's touching when someone's willing to sell you stuff at cost just to share the joy in blowing shit up, but nothing compares to the life-affirming zest of a guy who wants to teach you what he knows about building small bombs.

So Hugh and I became friends, in a difficult way where I was embarrassed to be seen hanging out with him. It isn't such a big thing if we're out in the train yards or on the edge of town, but I always worry that we'll be riding along, me on my black mountain bike and him on his racing bike with full fenders and saddle-bags, handlebars laden with lights and mirrors and a bell and a horn and a cycle-computer, and see Amanda Haldimand from school, who'd then forever think of me as the buddy of Hugh the King Nerd. That's not to be mean to Hugh, really, since he's just as desperate as I am to get a girlfriend and in a way he might even respect how I feel.

I look at the back of the house. The windows and door are tightly boarded, though the effects of the fire seem less visible here.

"I thought you said it'd be easy to get in," I say.

"It will be," says Hugh. "I checked earlier. Someone's already been in through the back door. We'll just pry 'em off."

"What, with our hands?" I ask, scoffing. The boards look pretty tightly fixed from where I'm standing: there are no visible gaps.

"With this," he says, unzipping the tote bag and brandishing a crowbar.

"Oh," I say.

"Let's get to work," Hugh says.

We cross the flagstone patio grown over with weeds; the closer we get to the house, the stronger the smell of smoke becomes. At first it smells like a fireplace, but after we've been there for a few minutes I notice beneath it the shadow stench of chemicals and tar.

I run my hand along the edge between the two sheets of particleboard nailed over the door. Then Hugh begins with the crowbar, wrenching the corners with surprising force and fighting to get the boards loose. He's right—someone has already been in. The boards are worn at the corners and I can see the marks of another crowbar on the doorframe underneath, but there are all kinds of nails and the boards are holding together well enough, squeaking and refusing to give. Hugh's really struggling. He finally gets the bottom board off and puts it on the ground. We both crouch down to look in.

What we can see of the house is black. It's far darker than I expected it was going to be—the missing board lets in a shaft of light no further than a few feet deep.

After we look in for a second, Hugh starts on the top board, which isn't budging at all.

"God damn it," he hisses.

"You want me to do it?" I ask.

"Sure," he says, handing me the crowbar. "You try a shift and I'll take over when you get tired."

The board isn't as tight as it looks, but it's got nails all the way along its length instead of just at the corners. Some of the nails seem fresher than others, so whoever came in nailed the board in better when they left. I wonder who that would have been—official people, cops or firefighters or insurance agents? The family? Imagine having to use a crowbar to break into your own burned-out house. What's worth going back for, and what are you going to do with what's left? If my house burned down I'd just want to leave everything in it behind and start again. What does it matter if it's all ruined anyway?

As I pull and lever at the board, Hugh says, "Hey, I got like an ounce of that really good weed I told you about."

"You got an *ounce*?" I say.

"Gotta spend my money on something," Hugh laughs with the same nasal honk he's always had.

After Hugh hooked me up with firecrackers, I felt I owed him a favour, so I smoked him up in his back yard one day after he tutored me. Weed was an instant hit with him, like something he'd been waiting for his whole life. For a while I'd get him a gram or two when I went over to my dealer's place, but for some reason I've been smoking less and less, so finally I just brought Hugh over to Casey's myself, and told Casey he was an okay dude. Since then he's been pretty much single-handedly paying Casey's rent and grocery bills on a monthly basis. Even though weed has less of a place in my life than ever, Hugh still goes on and on about it, maybe to show his appreciation, and every time we meet he makes a point of telling me about the quality of whatever he's been smoking, or of massive philosophical realizations he's come across while totally baked.

"And you'll never guess who I smoked it with on Tuesday," he adds with a tone of satisfied expectation, waiting for me to ask him to tell me more. I'm trying to get out a nail that seems to have no head but is stuck in the board anyway. Sweat is dripping down my temples in ticklish lines.

"Who's that?" I ask finally, hardly even aware that I've said it.

"Remember that girl I told you about?"

"The one from work?" I say. Hugh told me a month ago that this girl started working at the office of his dad's consulting company. When we talk about girls, it's unspoken that we both know Hugh's a geek with minimal social skills who wants nothing more than to get laid at long last. The discussions lately have become more desperate and I wonder if Hugh's undergoing some private crisis over his continuing lack of ass. Since this girl arrived at his job, he's been convinced that she might be the girl he finally gets to fuck and gives me updates about her every time we talk.

"Yeah," he says, "Ellen."

131

"Huh," I say with feigned interest. "You got high with Ellen."

Hugh pauses to build anticipation and waits too long. I stop crowbarring and turn around—he's smirking.

"*So,*" I repeat a little slower, "*You got high with Ellen?*"

Continuing to smirk, he replies, "I had *sex* with Ellen!"

"Whoa, what?" I say, surprised. "For real?"

"Totally."

"Huh!" I say. "Well, way to go. Congratulations." I return to working the crowbar.

"Thanks!" he says. "I invited her to come over and get high after work, and she did, and then we made dinner and watched a movie. Halfway through she just jumped on me. I hardly had to do anything."

"Wow," I say. "So it was, like, good?"

"Was it good!" he scoffs. "It was fucking *amazing.*"

"Great," I say. Only the left-hand side of the board is still nailed in. I'd just bend it back, but I'm pretty sure we'd end up getting stabbed to fuck by the dozens of nails sticking out of it. I start on the bottom corner.

"We did it in, like, every position," he says. "We started with her on top, but then we were all moving around and stuff."

The thought of Hugh doing anything naked is not appealing. I try to shut off his voice as he lists off rooms in his house, pieces of furniture, and bathroom products that the two managed to engage in their screwing. It's like he wants me to picture it—he's groping the air with his hands trying to tell me exactly how big her tits are, and doing this weird standing shuffle to tell me just how she moved her hips when she was riding him. As well, he keeps saying "the booty" when he talks about her ass. It's so much more than

132

I want to think about. Besides, even though he's older, it seems amazing and unfair to me that the King of the Nerds got laid before I did. Now there's this division between us where he's had sex and I haven't. He knows what that means and I don't.

I'm twisting and prying and pounding at the board that bars our entry. Finally I get it off, lean it against the wall of the house, hand the crowbar back to Hugh, and we look inside.

We're in the shade of a large tree in the neighbour's lot, so it's mostly dark. We can see two sets of stairs—one down into the basement, the other a short one leading up into the kitchen. Hugh steps into the darkness with one foot first to test his weight on the landing. I follow carefully. It's much colder than outside and that surprises me. The smell of smoke is so dense that it's creamy.

"You never know if it's burned through down below," Hugh's saying.

Hugh's spent more time in burn-outs than I have. For years before we started hanging out, he'd just ride around by himself, watching the trains and finding abandoned places to break into. So he always goes first.

"Is it safe for us to go in, you think?" I ask.

"Yeah," he says. "I don't think the fire was around here."

"Which way," I ask, "Up or down?"

"Let's try down first," Hugh says. He reaches into the tote bag, pulls out a flashlight about the length of a nightstick, and turns it on. The beam is strong and pure white. "You bring a flash?"

"No," I say, feeling stupid. "I didn't realize it'd be this dark. Anyway, I figured you'd have an extra."

Hugh rolls his eyes and digs around in the bag some more. "Well, I do, but you shouldn't *expect* it." Handing me the flashlight, he smiles that big brother smile he uses when he's teaching me something important. I turn the light on. It's a feeble orange spot that's more of a smudge than a beam, but it'll do.

Hugh's flashlight lights the stairs to the basement and he puts a foot down carefully on the top step. Sniffing the air, he tests his weight and the step groans. He puts a little more weight on it and it creaks louder.

"You smell that?" he asks. "Below the smoke? That's mould. Water damage. I'm not one hundred percent sure these stairs are safe."

We shine our flashlights around the basement and it doesn't seem like there's much down there anyway.

"Let's just go up," I say, strangely overeager and relieved that there's one fewer room to explore. We climb the four steps into the kitchen. It's then that I really smell the smoke and understand that we're here because the place, some-one's home, burned down.

The kitchen is totalled. The inside of the far wall is gone and underneath is all charred; what's left of the ceiling is smeared black and grey. Much of the wallboard and insulation from both is hanging down or on the floor in dirty piles—the charred support timbers are exposed and half-dissolved by fire. There had been shelves and a counter along that wall, but they're also on the floor, burned and broken. The linoleum is peeling up from the exposed parts of the floor, and there's a truly random collection of burned and scattered crap everywhere. I can't tell where it came from because it all seems so disconnected—dishtowels, auto-club maps, statuettes, a guitar case, a cracked power drill, a toy car, books, a lamp, a telephone handset, and framed photos. It's like someone's life went through a blender. I pull my shirt up over my face but it does nothing to counteract the immense reek of smoke.

Hugh is poking around slowly, looking at everything. He turns over a large framed photo and peers at it, angling his flashlight so it doesn't reflect. Then he says, "Come here, look at this."

I'm not sure if I want to. The more my eyes follow my peach-coloured flashlight beam around the ruined kitchen, the greater the sense I have that I'm trespassing in someone's life. But only what's left of it. I turn it over in my mind: people don't *live* here, they *lived* here. We're violating more than their home by breaking in: we've broken into the past, the dead.

"Seriously!" says Hugh, snapping me out of my morbid trance. "Look at this, it's a photo of the people who lived here."

I go over to where he's standing by the sink, and angle my flashlight across the cracked glass of the framed photo. The lower corners of the picture are singed, but what I can make out is a posed portrait of a family against a coloured backdrop. A man with a smooth helmet of hair and a moustache has his arm around the shoulder of a woman with short bob. She's holding a baby. They're looking the same direction, except the baby, who's staring blankly into space.

"They look fucked up," I say. "Look at their eyes."

"You can't even see their eyes!" Hugh says.

These are the people that lived here. They live somewhere else, I guess, if none of them died here.

"Listen, Hugh," I begin, my voice quiet again, "Do you know anything about the fire? Like, was everyone okay?

135

Did they get out?"

"I have no idea," says Hugh. "Why?"

"I don't know… It just feels weird to me here. Like, I don't want to be picking around a house where someone died. That's really fucked up."

"Well," Hugh says, "I don't have any reason to think anyone died here. I just figured they moved someplace else and haven't sold the house yet."

"I guess, eh?" I say.

"Are you afraid of ghosts?" Hugh asks. He's not goading, he's really asking. The fact that it's not a joke makes me nervous.

"No!" I say quickly. "I mean. Well—maybe. I've never been somewhere that I thought I'd have to be."

"Don't be. There's no reason. Plenty of houses burn every year. I'm sure these people"—he gestures at the photo—"were fine."

He trains his powerful light around the room for a second, then centres it on a melted blob hanging by wire from an intact portion of the ceiling.

"Look: they had smoke detectors!" He says this earnestly, genuinely wanting to convince me, but something about his tone irritates me. "They were safe. They got out."

I nod and we continue. We walk through the kitchen into the den. Its front half is badly damaged: the carpet has been rendered crunchy plastic, and the sofa and sitting chairs are black frames of black springs, half-buried under piles of debris. Dusty clumps of wall and insulation and burned wood once again cover everything.

There's a large TV in the back corner. The screen is fogged and seems to be cracked on the inside. Above the TV there are a bunch of movies on videotape that have warped in the heat but didn't burn. They don't tell me much about the people who watched them: *Indiana Jones*, *Barney*, *Batman*, *Gone with the Wind*, and *The Best of Saturday Night Live* could belong to anybody. I realize that I'm looking for evidence of who the people who lived here were, and it feels shamefully pornographic, but the disgust doesn't stop me. Hugh's digging at something in the corner.

"What have you got?" I ask.

"Nothing much. Some old porcelain stuff. It's cracked and sooty, but I figure I'll grab it and see what it's like when I clean it up."

There are some scorched books on the shelf above the TV. I pick one large book up. It feels crumbly in my hands, but holds together as I gently open it to the middle and look. It's some sort of coffee-table souvenir of a 1970s musical. There are makeup-lacquered actors posed in mock wonder, glee, and excitement against a sterile prop backdrop, their immense bouffant hair like clown wigs. I turn a few pages, mostly stuck together, and the spine cracks. Suddenly, I feel terribly sad and put the book back as Hugh signals me with his flashlight that we should move on.

I don't want to continue, but I'm afraid to tell that to Hugh, especially now that he thinks I'm afraid of ghosts. That's not it at all, but I don't want to start talking about it, so I follow him, no longer saying much. It takes a while to go up the stairs, because he wants to check each one so we don't fall through.

At the top we find a hallway with three doors. The first is the bathroom, which is mostly empty except for a few muddy facecloths and towels on the floor. Across the hall we find the master bedroom.

It's badly done-in. There's a high burned bed with crisp posts that have fallen like matchsticks, two dressers with the drawers open, and half-burned clothes strewn about the black and hardened carpet.

One of the dressers isn't badly damaged, so Hugh fights to open the one closed drawer and shines his flashlight in. I watch him, wondering about what it was like to live here, and what it would be like to have to get up suddenly and run out of my house, never to return. If it was my house, I think, maybe it'd be different. Maybe it would give me a clean start, but maybe it would take the last of all the good things down with it. Out of the dresser, Hugh pulls a large pair of white men's briefs, smudged with soot, and waves them at me. I force a smile.

Needing something to do, I look through the drawers in the scorched dresser nearest me. The outside is burned, but the inside isn't as bad and has been mostly emptied except for a few items of clothing which I don't feel like examining further. I notice a tube of ointment in the corner of the drawer, pull it out, and shine my flash on it. It's *Anusol*, the existence and use of which Hugh, in another moment of worldliness, recently explained to me. I pull it out and show it to him.

"What's that?" he says. He's craning his neck to follow the flash beam into a middle drawer that wouldn't open all the way.

"*Anusol*," I say. Hugh guffaws.

"No way," he says. "Really?"

"For real," I say.

He laughs harder. "Hey," he says, "Maybe I should take that. I get the feeling that Ellen might be needing it soon enough."

I'm not actually sure what he means by that, except that he's having sex with someone and I'm not, and that takes me away from the immediately weird scenario of being inside someone's ruined bedroom and reminds me that I'm sixteen and it's sunny outside, even if I'm in here. Even if Hugh, the King of the Nerds, can get laid.

"You get anything good?" I ask.

"Perfume bottles," he says, inspecting the top drawer of the dresser and withdrawing something else.

"What's that?" I say.

"Nothing," he says.

"Lemme see, then."

Hugh awkwardly disagrees for a second, then sheepishly pulls out a of pair of worn black panties from his bag. It's reassuring to know that even if he got to fuck Ellen, he's still creepy.

But it's also not reassuring. I watch Hugh stuff the underwear into his bag and feel disgusted. These people, whoever they were, never intended for some kid to be pawing through their bedroom, snatching their underwear to use for something awful later on. This was the secret centre of these people's lives—they slept and fucked here, they dressed and undressed. They had this room and then they lost it, so we decided it belonged to us. This thought is cold inside me as we return to the hall.

The last doorway is across from the grown-up room. I'd be happy just to quit and leave without opening it, but we're exploring, and this is what we do. Hugh leads, as always, and I follow close behind him because I'm afraid of the darkness behind me even more than what's in front.

The photo downstairs must have been old, because in the baby's room there's no crib, only a small bed. The mattress is burned black, but the headboard and footboard are still standing. Long strips have been torn out of the wall beside the bed, leaving it open to the crisp timbers, and insulation is littered throughout the room. The lamp next to the bed has a circus-themed porcelain base dusted grey and black, and there are burned children's books and blackened stuffed animals on the floor. I feel myself growing dizzy. My hand finds the wall beside me, but it's dusty-wet with mould and the wallpaper underneath is heat-crinkled and shrunk. I snap my hand away and wipe it vigorously across the leg of my pants, over and over.

Against the opposite wall, Hugh's examining a white piggy bank, shaking and peering at it in the blast of his flashlight beam. I slowly creep my own beam across the floor again, looking at the burned pieces of plush animals, the cardboard early-reader books, the mobile of glass farm animals arrayed around a barn. I feel myself seized with a panicked, terrified wonder. Why is this stuff still here? Why didn't someone come and take it away? Someone's already been here for some of the things, but what about the rest of it? This was someone's life. For the kid who lived here, this room was the whole world. Why is any of it left?

"Come on, man," I say to Hugh.

"Jussec," he says.

"No," I say. "Let's get the hell out of here. I don't feel right."

"Don't be a chicken," he says. "It's fine. Nobody died here."

"Fucking come *on*," I whine. He's still digging. I take two sharp steps toward him and shove him into the dresser. He stumbles, then spins and blinds me with his huge flash-light.

"What the fuck was that for?" he says in his affronted King Nerd voice, and I'm full of hate for him. Instantly I remember who I am and who he is.

"I said let's go," I announce, my voice deeper and thicker than before. "I want to get out of here. This isn't right. You're digging through a little kid's piggy bank, for Christ's sake."

"I didn't take anything," he says.

"Come on, man, let's go," I say, listening to my own voice and trying to speak slowly. "This is fucked up."

"You can go if you want," he says. "I'll come when I'm done."

The truth is that I don't want to find my way back down through the house alone. I don't know what I think is waiting there, but I'm sure I can feel it. He finally closes the drawer and turns to me.

"Okay," he says, "We can go if you want to."

"About fucking time," I say, but my voice isn't as steady as it was.

"What's gotten into you, man?" he says. "Are you okay?"

The tone of Hugh's voice startles me, and I wonder if maybe there's nothing frightening in the house, if maybe what's wrong is inside me. The house I can leave, but if I go crazy, I can never escape. I can't even think about that.

"Come on," I say.

"Okay, man, chill out," he says, following me.

Down the stairs, we pass the den and kitchen once more, and finally I see the glorious white light pounding into the darkness through the door to the backyard.

As we emerge into the blinding heat of daylight, there's a stillness in the overgrown lot that feels ominous, as though somehow the product of a conspiracy to make everything seem alright. It should feel alright, I think. There's no reason why it shouldn't. Yet the buzzing of the cicadas and the listless rustle of wind puffing through the saggy leaves seem rehearsed and nervous. There's something I'm doing wrong, I think, something that I know that I'm not supposed to.

"Hey man," I say as we step outside, pushing myself to be normal again.

Hugh turns to face me impatiently.

"I'm sorry for shoving you. I just got to feeling real weird in there. I don't know what it was. I got to feeling we were doing something bad."

"Well," he says, "We weren't. No one lives here. This place is like a huge pile of garbage that was too big to take to the curb. We can pick through it—there's nothing wrong with that."

"No," I said, "I know, I know. It's just me, I realize. I just started feeling kind of weird. I'm sorry. I shouldn't have shoved you."

"Alright," he says. "It's cool."

I extend my hand.

Hugh nods, accepts it, then puts down his bags and removes a small hammer from the knapsack. Together we nail the boards back up over the door. I try to find the holes where the nails were before and it makes the job quieter, but even then the dull tapping and accepting of the hammer and wood seems like it's being played through a PA system throughout the neighbourhood.

I'm nervous, but sealing the hole shut makes me very happy. It's like nailing a coffin lid down. When I was younger I was shocked to learn that coffins got their lids nailed shut. I wondered what would happen if the person inside needed to get out, or if, for whatever reason, people outside needed to get in. Only after I thought it over did it make sense, like it does here.

We wait a while after we finish before heading into the street.

"What'd you get?" I ask him as we lean against the house. "Anything good?"

"Not sure," he says. "A bunch of old tin boxes, some bottles. Whoever lived there must have collected them."

"You think they'll blow up good?" I ask.

"There are a few things that look promising," he replies. "You wanna come over and get high? I made some new devices last night. We can see how those perfume bottles go up."

"Yeah," I say, "Why not? Sure."

After a few minutes of waiting, Hugh insists I go ahead to check that the scene is clear. I inch up out of the musty shade of the driveway into the corner of the front lawn. There's nothing moving on the street and all is still in the houses across the way. I slowly follow the tangled hedge that skirts the driveway to the sidewalk and peek around it. Our bikes are still locked to the signpost, and there's no indication that anything has changed since we arrived.

Yet as I stand at the hedge and watch the street, my pulse grows quick and dominant in my chest and neck and ears. The stillness of the air unnerves me—there isn't anything happening anywhere and I wonder desperately why. I wish there was just one lawnmower droning, or a hammer other than my own—any signal of upkeep, construction, or the presumption of a future—I wish so hard that I practically ache, but for nothing. There's just silence, doomed and irreparable. I think again of how sinister it is that the suburbs came out this far and then just stopped.

My sweaty hands are knotted into themselves, fingernails biting the flesh of my palms, and I've begun to breathe in little reverse-barks with my heart tapping my chest accusingly. I imagine how for a while people lived here, waiting happily for the city to follow and swallow them up, but it never happened, and instead the place began to crumble, people got diseases, died, and it became unspoken that the experiment had failed. Like everything is going to fail.

Then I hear Hugh approaching. I unclench my hands, take a long, slow breath, and turn around.

"All clear," I say, trying to sound as though I mean it. "Let's go."

Anna Leventhal

Epilogue: The Land and How it Lied

Look at the map.

How much do you remember, after all? The smell of the nape of someone's neck, the way a particular tree cast a shadow on your bare calf. The air conditioners on your neighbour's roof, and how they looked like the skyline of a faraway city. The way the potholes on Main Street opened up onto cobblestone and made you think of your great-grandmother and her lover riding curtained from a hotel tryst. You remember things you weren't even sure you lived through, like the fire at the ladder workshop or the time those kids snuck into the abandoned house to make kissy-face and had the roof fall in on their heads. You lived here, and you thought that made you a pretty big deal, like all your collected experience added up something special, some kind of stamp or seal with your name on it in cursive. You lived here! And that should count for something, right?

But here, from above, everything looks uniformly beige, and smaller than you remember it. Was your house really so close to the river? It seemed to take forever for the water to rise up to the front steps, the way you hoped it would when you were a kid during the flood. But now everything looks so tidy, you can't even tell where the paths used to be. People, the living, cover the place like foam, and really you're all about as durable. In the end what remains is the land, and some stories of how it lay.

Bios

Adam Bobbette lives and works in Montréal and sometimes in other places.

Sue Carter Flinn is an award-winning journalist and arts editor for *The Coast*, Halifax's alt-weekly newspaper. Her story *Catechism* appeared in the Invisible anthology *Transits*.

Raised in Calgary, **Dan Gillean** can now be found slinging eggs and coffee around the various diners of Montréal when he is not writing.

Stephen Guy is a member of the Wolfe Island Ferry Story Cabal.

Wasela Hiyate is a Toronto writer who has lived and travelled in Europe, Asia and the Caribbean, working as everything from waitress to ESL teacher to television producer. While in the University of British Columbia's MFA Creative Writing program, she completed a collection of stories about travel, cultural alienation and the global economy. Some of these stories are forthcoming in the anthology *TOK 3: Writing the New Toronto* and *Descant Magazine*. Her work has been published in Canadian literary magazines such as *The Malahat Review*, *Grain* and *The New Quarterly*. She is currently negotiating the mysteries of martial arts and the process of writing a novel—both violently enlightening endeavours.

Anna Leventhal's fiction has appeared in *Geist* and will be published in the forthcoming anthology *Journey Prize Stories 20* from McClelland & Stewart. She has created experimental radio works, experimental performance pieces, and lately, an experimental garden. She lives in Montréal.

Molly Lynch is a writer who divides her time between Montréal and the backwoods of British Columbia. Her stories often reinterpret myth and legend in contemporary contexts. *In Public* draws on childhood memories of healthy cereal and the discovery of hairspray. She is presently finishing her first novel.

Sean Michaels lives in Montréal, Québec. Sometimes he writes about music for the *National Post*, *The Believer*, and at saidthegramophone.com. He is available for engagement parties, picnics and sweet sixteens.

For the past twelve years **Jeff Miller** has written and published *Ghost Pine Fanzine*, an annual collection of autobiographical stories. He is also a founding member of the Soul Gazers writers group and the sporadic Trash Can Lit reading series. He lives in Montréal.

J.B. Staniforth grew up in Ottawa and lives in Montréal, where he teaches literature to indifferent college students. Between 2001 and 2004 he published eight issues of the personal/literary zine *Querencia*; since that time he has written a novel, *Dread*, and a collection of short stories, *Passenger Side*, both of which he is currently editing.

Michelle Sterling lives and writes in Montréal. She has been published in *Maisonneuve* and *Matrix*.

Vincent Tinguely is a Montréal writer and performance poet. He is the co-author of *Impure—reinventing the word*, a book about the Montréal spoken word scene. He regularly writes about spoken word and literary events for the free weekly *Montréal Mirror*. His work has recently appeared in *Four Minutes to Midnight no. 9*.

Teri Vlassopoulos lives and writes in Montréal, Québec. She has been making zines for over ten years and is currently working on a novel.

Invisible Publishing is committed to working with writers who might not ordinarily be published and distributed commercially. We work exclusively with emerging and under-published authors to produce entertaining, affordable, print-based art.

We believe that books are meant to be enjoyed by everyone and that sharing our stories is important. In an effort to ensure that books never become a luxury, we do all that we can to make our books more accessible.

We are collectively organized, our production processes are transparent. At Invisible, publishers and authors recognize a commitment to one another, and to the development of communities which can sustain and encourage storytellers.

If you'd like to know more please get in touch.
info@invisiblepublishing.com

Invisible Publishing
Halifax & Montréal